# FRANK

Julie Hamill

*Frank* is a work of fiction. Names, characters,
places, events and incidents are either the products
of the author's imagination or used in a fictitious
manner. Any resemblance to actual persons, living
or dead, or actual events is purely coincidental.
Some Airdrie locations have been used for settings.
All locations stem from the author's fond memories
of living in Airdrie as a girl aged 9-17

Cover photo: 'Frank' (Jimmy Hamill)
'young Jackie' (Rose Ann Hamill)

ISBN-13: 978-0-9956495-7-6

Saron Publishing
Pwllmeyrick House
Mamhilad
Mon
NP4 8RG

saronpublishers.co.uk

Follow us on Facebook or Twitter

'No half parties.'

# CONTENTS

| 1 | Carry on Surviving | 7 |
| 2 | Sugar Feet | 24 |
| 3 | A Better Father | 37 |
| 4 | Tea Bags | 47 |
| 5 | Sunday Lunch | 58 |
| 6 | A June Birthday | 70 |
| 7 | Move It | 82 |
| 8 | Guardian Angels | 94 |
| 9 | Granda's Pride | 108 |
| 10 | Going Up | 120 |
| 11 | Trouble | 130 |
| 12 | Yes, Dear | 143 |
| 13 | The Kiss | 154 |
| 14 | Shut The Door | 170 |

# CARRY ON SURVIVING

Frank slid the new white shirt and sky blue tie set out of the packet, carefully unfolded the sleeves and removed all the little plastic clips. He placed them in a neat bundle on the bedside table. The shirt creases were visible at the shoulders, chest, elbows and waist, but he planned to wear a jacket over the top so it wouldn't need an iron. Jackie bought the shirt for him for Christmas last year, but he'd never had occasion to wear it. In fact, he forgot he had it until he had to clear some clothes out a few months ago.

He shaved his face systematically and absentmindedly: upper lip, chin, cheek, other cheek, neck. He combed what was left of his hair across the top of his head, patting and flattening the rest down at the sides with shaving water. A few dabs of *Mesmerise* momentarily stung his skin while he put his clothes on. Polished shoes were the final touch before he went downstairs to present himself to June, his wife of forty years, where she would make her usual minor adjustments to his tie and brush his shoulders.

June's customary inspection of what he wore was

something he enjoyed. He liked all compliments, from anyone willing to give them, but June's compliments always made him feel an inch taller. He was proud of how they looked together. He was proud of how she carried herself. He loved that she still turned heads and looked younger and slimmer than other women her age. Now in her sixties, she still made the effort to look attractive. She avoided cream cakes, sweets and chocolate, despite the new trend of elasticated waists on the fifty-plus age group.

Tonight she wore a fitted black skirt with a kick pleat and a cream blouse with a Peter Pan collar, one of his favourite looks. He watched as she put on her shoes and popped a comb and a can of hairspray in her bag, then tapped the side pocket; her signal that she was ready to go. He escorted her out of the front door, locked it and put the key in his pocket. They linked arms and began their Friday evening walk to the Working Men's Club, under a wave of light drizzle.

The sun had been out that morning but had disappeared at around twelve o'clock to make way for the day's rain. On the odd summer afternoon when it was fine and bright, all local men rushed to remove shirts and vests, sit on their back garden step and smile. Drinking in enough of the sun's fiery light was essential, and the heat felt glorious on the skin. A burnt back or crimson forearm was a badge of the highest boast. Men were often seen in the streets pointing to their own peeling bald heads as evidence that there really had been a scorcher the week before.

Frank lifted his chin and strode through the inclement weather, just as his mother told him to all those years ago.

'Do you no harm,' she'd say, and she was right.

There was no point bringing an umbrella; June had lost dozens in the Club in the past. His dampened jacket would dry on his back in seconds, the hot smoky air of the Working Men's Club would see to that. June would fix her hair in the Ladies toilet as soon as they arrived, or my God, would he hear about the frizz. He noticed that two of her carefully tonged curls had begun to straighten as they reached the end of the road, so he quickened the pace.

Frank walked with purpose. He liked to take everything in, even sights he had seen a hundred times before. New shops, old shops, the baths; anybody up to no good, anybody with a new hair do. Fresh graffiti at the bus stop - 'SHUGIE!' - did he know that name? To Frank, these types of discoveries were akin to finding a shiny fifty pence piece on the pavement and pocketing it. *Somebody dropped that. It's mine now.*

He thrived on noticing changes before anybody else, like that time he found out they were knocking down the old cinema to build a supermarket. He told everybody. A year later, he was down the front at the ribbon cutting.

Turning the corner to the street that the Club was on, he saw a dog sniffing at a lamppost, a young man staggering with a bag of chips, and a few boys playing Kick The Can around the empty market car park. The boys had no jackets on, lost in their play. *Looks like a good game*, he smiled to himself, then a sudden thought struck him.

'June, did we bring the washing in? I don't remember bringing in the washing.'

June smiled and shrugged. He searched his mind, trying to remember unpegging clothes, and it bothered him that he couldn't remember. He wanted to know, or for June to answer. Maybe she didn't know. Sometimes she talked, sometimes she didn't. That's just the way it was. They crossed the road towards the Working Men's Club.

'Maybe our Jackie brought it in,' he mumbled, as they approached the entrance. 'Be okay. It was towels anyway, I think.'

It was Frank's first night back at the Club in a

while. He wasn't sure about going, but his daughter Jackie had insisted he meet her new boyfriend, Tommy, and Frank promised he'd go along and have a drink with them. He wanted to meet Tommy anyway, as he had heard from Bobby that Tommy had a reputation for tearing through women like packets of crisps.

As they neared the top of the slope to the front door of the Club, June paused to remove a lipstick from her bag. She popped the lid off, smiled at Frank, and dabbed it all around the corners and rubbed her lips together. It was applied expertly and perfectly, without a mirror. She clicked the lid back on and put the lipstick back in her bag. She used a tissue to blot her slightly wet cheeks and under her eyes.

It was like she was really there, in front of him. He could see her clearly.

But her funeral was six months ago.


The first time he saw her, she appeared by the kitchen sink, scrubbing burnt potatoes off the bottom of the pot.

I told you to turn them down to a gas 3, he heard her say, while she looked directly into the suds. Frank retreated to the living room and sat, cold in his chair, his fingers gripping the wooden arms like claws. He stayed there until she was gone.

A few days later, she was in the bedroom folding clothes and putting socks into drawers. `You could do with a few more black pairs, these ones have seen better days`, she said. Frightened by another vision, he hurried to the bathroom, clicked the lock to red and washed his face. He sat down on the edge of the bath and waited there until he thought she was gone.

In the past few weeks, her visits had gone from occasionally to daily. Normally when Jackie was at work in the hospital, always when he was alone. June would appear, sitting where she used to sit on the couch, or she'd appear when nobody seemed to be looking, then disappear, without explanation. She liked to comment on what he was watching on TV, just like she did when she was alive.

`Change it, that's rubbish!`

Once, she appeared beside him in a crowded betting shop while he was placing a bet on a horse.

`Jimmy's chance? No chance! Stick a fiver on this one - The Swanky Dazzler.`

These days she was everywhere, a running commentary beside his own thoughts, like two cars on a Scalextric track. She answered his questions, pointed out his faults, laughed at his little remarks, chastised the little chubby one on *Dallas* and accompanied him to the shop. He could see her, but Jackie couldn't. He could hear her, but Jackie couldn't. Once, he asked Jackie if he saw her in the garden, but she didn't seem to understand.

'Did you see your mammy there, out the window, by the white rose bush?'

'Aye, I know what you mean, I can just imagine her.'

As time passed, he found it a comfort to have June's ghost, or whatever it was, around him. Feeling her near gave him the confidence to behave like his old self, and helped to shelve his grief for another day. When she was first gone, he had to try to learn how to be 'in charge' of himself, a severed half of what used to be. He pushed himself to carry on. Carry on shaving. Carry on and get the Hoover out. Carry on dressing. Just carry on.

He always thought she'd outlive him, and that they had at least another twenty years together. He worried that, in the end, she had suffered. Right after the funeral, he spent days thinking of her last days in the hospice, of the pain and the crying.

'This is the end, Frank, it's the end,' she'd whisper, her voice barely perceptible.

'Don't say that! You'll outlive us all!' he lied through tears.

After her funeral, when the mourners left and the

last hot toddy glass had been washed, things went quiet again. He sat in his chair facing the television, pushing the power button on and off with a walking stick he'd found in a skip. He liked to hear the music of *Coronation Street*. He liked to try to remember nice things. Like the day he got the phone call at work to say that June was pregnant. At forty-three, she was having the baby they thought would never be. The next day, his pals at work threw him a party with T-bone steaks and fried eggs for lunch. They washed the steak down with bottles of brown ale, then went back to work on the railway tracks.

He liked to look at her picture on the mantelpiece every day. It had been taken at a wedding some years back. She was dressed glamorously in a lemon suit and matching hat that had a navy brim. She'd had a few glasses of champagne and looked relaxed and happy. In the picture, she stared off into the distance, her lips smiling sweetly. Frank always wondered what she was looking at.

Behind this picture, there was another picture of them dancing at the Working Men's Club. They had been going every Friday night, since they were young. They were nicknamed 'the salt and pepper pots', because one was rarely seen without the other. They sat together, danced together and talked together. They never danced with anyone else. Outside of the Club, they went to Fine Fare together, stood in the queue for Airdrie Savings Bank together, went to twelve o'clock Mass together, and collected his pension together after Frank retired.

He found going to church very difficult. He had never noticed before, but the hymns all seemed to be about dying. *Lord, I have heard you calling in the night... Come, follow me, and I will give you rest / Blest are you that weep and mourn for one day you will laugh.* So he stopped going to Mass. The Post Office queue seemed to take much longer, and, not knowing what to buy without June's instructions, he left the food shopping to Jackie. Jackie did almost everything after the funeral, while he sat in his chair, silent and staring. But Jackie was hardly at home now since she met Tommy, and Frank had noticed a coating of dust on his bedside table that morning.

Standing outside the Club, he swallowed away the past. June wouldn't want this. As he pushed the door, he knew she would disappear, and she did.

Once inside the main door, he made his way through the smoke and noise to get to a stool at the end of the bar. He sat down, smiled and said hello with as much nicety as he could manage and ordered a drink.

'Hi, Bobby. I'll take a pint when you're ready.'

'Hello, Frank! Nice to see you back! Is that the rain off?'

'Ach... It's kind of on and off.'

'How's things with you... all right?' he asked gently, pulling down on the Tennent's Special tap, the foamy beer rushing to fill the glass.

'Aye, struggling away, you know.'

Bobby settled the pint on the beer mat marked *Quizzer!* as he continued, 'I can imagine. It's good to see you.' The head of the beer slid down the side of the pint and Frank rushed to sup it up.

'Is our Jackie in yet?' he asked, changing the subject. He didn't want Bobby's sad chat. He took a sip of the beer and placed 85p on the bar. 'Is she in with that Tommy, have you seen?' Bobby took the money and rung up the till. He paused and looked back at Frank.

'If you mean, Tommy Fletcher, she is, yes.' He shut the till. 'I have to tell you, Frank,' Bobby motioned for Frank to lean in, 'Seemingly...I don't mean to talk out of turn about your Jackie, but that Tommy has been seen hanging around with a lassie from the button factory...'

'I've heard. Quality Control Maureen?'

'Aye - Quality Control Maureen, QCM.' Frank took a few gulps of his pint as he listened to Bobby. 'And she's old enough to be his granny! He must have ran out of women his mammy's age! Except for your Jackie, of course...whom he's very lucky to have.'

'What I want to know is, how can Jackie not see him for what he is-'

Bobby interrupted Frank by tapping his arm and nodding towards the dance floor. Frank spun round on his stool. Jackie's arms were draped around Tommy Fletcher, swaying to *Tonight's The Night* by Rod Stewart.

A big crowd of women in their fifties and sixties burst through the door, and, despite the slower-paced music, formed a conga around the dance floor wearing a glitter of black sparkle and luminous Lycra.

'Oh, no... speak of the devil...here come the button busters...' said Bobby, with his eyes on the door, watching woman after woman dance in, each with a smile, laugh or wave for the Club-goers at the other tables.

The Button Factory ladies shimmied over to the seated area and pushed two tables together. They put £5 notes in an empty pint glass in the middle. Three stayed at the table putting coats onto grabbed chairs and the rest continued dancing. Some of them pushed past Frank and shouted to Bobby.

'Bobby! Bobby! Make us Tequila Sunrises! Bobby! Tequila Sunrises! Have you got tequila?'

'I've got tequila, aye, but bloody sunrise? What the heck is that? Limeade not do you?'

'No! It has to be red and yella! Red and yella!'

'Hold on, I suppose I can have a go, I've got that red lemonade somewhere.' Some of the women cheered. Frank tut-tutted, and put his pint down. He glanced at Jackie who was still dancing. He motioned to Bobby to keep an eye on his pint and went off to the toilet. When he returned, the one known as Quality Control Maureen was sitting on his stool and shouting: 'Mary! Mary! Get us a vodka, Mary! No! No! Mary! I don't like that stuff! No! It's too juicy! Sickly! A vodka! Aye!'

Frank looked to the dance floor. Jackie had moved to a nearby table with Tommy Fletcher and a few of the crowd that hung around his betting shop. He looked back to his seat to see that Maureen was still sitting on it. Feeling slightly put out - everybody knew this was his stool - he motioned at her to move.

'Shift.'

'What's that, gorgeous? Aye! I'll take a drink off you, no bother!'

'That's my seat. Everybody in here knows it.'

'The two of us can sit on it!' She winked and patted her knee. Frank scowled at her, lifted his pint and squeezed back through the crowd, avoiding lit cigarettes on his best suit jacket.

'Dad! Dad! Here! Dad!' Jackie shouted, now sitting on Tommy Fletcher's knee. 'Sit here, Dad, next to us. There's loads of room. Tommy - get that seat. No, that one. There's nobody on it. Just put the coat on the floor. Dad! Sit here! Pull the seat over a bit, Tommy. Over a bit more. Pull it! Dad, sit here.'

'That's somebody's seat,' said Frank.

'No, it isn't, there was nobody on it.'

'There was a coat on it!'

'There was not. Shhh! Dad, this is Tommy. Tommy, this is my dad.'

'Hello, Mister McNeill, or should I call you Frank?'

Tommy was dressed in a tight mod suit and skinny tie, his hair perfectly combed back, shiny but greasy at the same time. Jackie, the apple of Frank's eye, was tall and slender, her hair styled in a short brown bob, a triangle of freckles dotted across her nose. She looked too good for Tommy; too pure. Frank knew it, everybody knew it, but he had to make the effort, for her.

'You can call me Frank. Frank is fine. Pleased to meet you.'

'I'm just getting drinks, want anything?'

Frank looked to his pint to see half was left.

'I'll take a pint off you, thanks very much.'

Watching Tommy until he got two-deep into the bar, Frank turned to Jackie, who had moved to her own stool, and was bobbing her head to *Precious* by The Jam.

'Jackie,'

'What?'

'Is he not a bit...'

'Who?'

'Him. Is he not a bit...he's been out with everybody, Jackie.'

'He's all right, Dad. Don't worry. We're getting on magic. He says he's going to take me to see his pal's band after a few drinks here. Says they're nearly signed. We'd be on the guest list, Dad - hardly anybody gets on the guest list. They're supposed to be amazing. Seemingly, Archie Wilson is going.'

'Archie Wilson from The Feathers?'

'No. Archie Wilson! The music guy!'

'Do I know him?'

'You don't know everybody, Dad. He's a talent spotter from a record company.'

'Oh, aye.' Frank finished the last of his pint and

shouted over the music, 'Jackie. Jackie! Listen. The thing is, well, he's a lot older than you... what do you think your mum would say?' He nodded towards Tommy who was getting served at the bar.

Jackie looked Frank in the eye and downed her drink.

'Aye...well she's not here, is she?' replied Jackie, a flash of green crossing her eyes like a shock of lightning. 'I'm twenty-one, dad. I'm a big girl now.'

Tommy returned with a tray of fresh drinks. He set it down on the table and turned to talk to a big redheaded guy who was standing further down towards the bar. The two flat-headed beers had made a puddle on the tray. Jackie took her vodka from the tray and beer dripped off the bottom of it. She looked at Frank mischievously and wiped the bottom of the glass on Tommy's seat cushion, then took the two pints and did the same. Frank shook his head at her and laughed.

'Stop that! He'll catch you when his arse gets wet!' he laughed. She giggled and they both took sips as the music changed.

'I love this song! Come and dance, Dad!'

'No, hen. I'm just on my second pint. I'm not dancing yet.'

'Tommy! Tommy! C'mon, dance!' Jackie shouted, 'It's *Lion Sleeps To-night*,' she sang. 'Come on!'

'Aye, right!' Tommy nudged his redheaded pal. He looked to Jackie, and shouted, 'What are the odds of me dancing to that crap?' He laughed and the redheaded one did a hula dance. Jackie went off to the dance floor on her own, knocking against other dancers, taking the central space to wave her arms around.

He could hear June.

Look after her, Frank.

'I will.'

Don't let her drink too much.

'I won't.'

Go and dance with her.

'I wish people would stop telling me to dance.'

Bobby the barman's voice crackled over the music: 'Just a few more songs before The Mac takes over for amateur hour. If you fancy doing a wee turn, put your name down on The Mac's clipboard.' The announcement ended abruptly as Bobby put the microphone down on the bar without switching it off, causing a howl of feedback. Everybody plugged their ears until it calmed. The music came back on abruptly and The Mac raised the clipboard over his head, stretching himself up to his full height of five foot four.

Jackie rushed back over to Frank.

'Dad! Are you putting your name down? What'll

you sing? Are you going to sing *Pizza Pie*?'

'You mean, *That's Amore*?'

'Aye. *That's Amore*. Are you going to do it, Dad? Please!'

'Oh, all right, then. Go and put my name down.'

'Yes!' She leapt up, delighted, and rushed off to find a pen. Frank looked around to see Tommy talking to Maureen. Tommy's thumb and forefinger rested on the space at the back of the bar stool, near her waist.

# SUGAR FEET

Jackie staggered towards the taxi rank, holding onto Tommy's arm.

'I saw you talking to her!'

'You're drunk.'

'I might be a tiny bit tiddly, but I saw you.'

'Hurry up. Walk straight! And don't be sick in the taxi this time.' Tommy opened a car door and pushed Jackie into the back of the taxi. 'Crown Estate,' he said to the driver. He rummaged in his pocket, finding a receipt and a one pound note and some change.

'Give me your bag, we need to pay the man.' Jackie grabbed her bag and threw it at him.

'Watch it!' he threatened.

'Watch what? You and that tart from the button factory? I saw you, slabbering all over her at the toilets. Disgusting. Like a big slabbery dog... slabberin.' Jackie leaned her head against the window and closed her eyes.

'I want to go to see the band...you said Archie Wilson...'

Tommy took a few pounds from Jackie's purse, then threw the bag back at her.

'Not happening.'

He turned and looked out of his window. The car stopped at the lights next to the chip shop. Tommy saw Maureen, laughing with her friend Isla, an open bag of chips in one hand, wooden fork in the other. Seeing Tommy, Isla nudged Maureen's elbow and Maureen paused, chip to mouth. Tommy stared and nodded. He held her glance until the lights changed and the car drove away.

Frank started singing as he put the key in the back door.

'...*Tippi tippi tay...Tippi tippi tay...Like a gay tarantella.*' He hiccupped. 'Gay...nice wee word, that.' He hiccupped again as he shut the door and locked it behind him. 'That's me in, hen,' he shouted. He glanced upstairs and paused for an answer. 'Shhh! She's in her bed,' he said to himself in the hall mirror, and then tiptoed back through to the kitchen. He flicked the kettle on, and it flicked off again. He ambled towards the tap and filled it up, then flicked the kettle back on. He opened the fridge and took out the milk.

'Where's the eggs?' he shouted, staring into the fridge. He shut the fridge door, then walked into the living room and sat down in his chair. He strained to pull his shoes off. He removed his socks and threw them one by one to the other side of the room like an over-tired toddler. He rubbed his feet and glanced to June's photo on the mantelpiece.

'Are you coming to visit me tonight?' He paused and looked to her place on the couch. 'It was a good night. I'm glad I went, you were right. That Rough Isla was in; she's a great laugh. Bobby calls her *The Isla Rough*, that tickles me, that. She's not that rough! Och, it was just fun. We've no eggs, by the way. I'm starving. There's not a morsel in that fridge.' He heard the kettle click off.

'Kettle's boiled,' he said, as he got up to go into the kitchen. The cold lino sent a shudder right up through from his feet to the back of his neck. He yelped, dancing around. 'Are my slippers in there?' He stood still, waiting to hear a response. 'This floor's like an ice rink.'

Receiving no reply, he grabbed two tea towels and dropped them to the floor. He put a foot on each towel and tried to ski across the floor to the counter. As he reached for a tea bag, his shirtsleeve caught on the sugar packet and knocked it across the counter, spilling sugar all across the worktop, showering down onto the floor like confetti.

'Oh, no! I'm for it!'

He took the dry cloth from the sink taps and flicked some sugar back into the sink. He put milk in the tea, then skied back across the floor until he reached the carpet. The tea splashed over the side of the cup. He sat back down in front of the TV and, unable to reach his stick, leaned over to change the channels as he sipped tea. Pleasantly surprised to find the fight scene in *The Quiet Man*, he leaned back into the cushion and rested the hot mug on the wooden chair handle.

'Aye, this is a good bit.'

He began to watch John Wayne pull Maureen O'Hara by the arm and smiled gently at the screen. He took June's picture from the mantelpiece and ran his index finger over her hair in the frame.

'I'd never drag you by the arm, it was always linked to mine. Are you coming to see me tonight? I miss you. I'm useless. Can't do anything. I don't know if you're really visiting me or if I'm seeing things, but I don't mind. Jackie, she can't see you but I can see you. Why can I see you? I love seeing you now. I don't know where Jackie went. You'd know if you were here. Why did you have to go, June?' He yawned. 'Why did you have to leave...me' Frank's head lolled and his eyes closed as he drifted into sleep in his chair.

It's all right, Frank, it's me. June was standing above him, stroking his head. He looked up at her.

'Am I dreaming?' he asked.

I'm here, for now. I'm here, she replied.


The metal heels of Maureen's worn down stilettos echoed through the dark close as she staggered along, poking her fork into the last few chips. A tall, slim shadow was leaning by her front door. She knew who it was; not a black hair out of place, slim-fit suit, skinny tie, and one hand in his left trouser pocket. A smile crept across her mouth as she walked closer, crumpled up the chip paper and threw it down. Maureen liked the way he looked at her, like he was ready to devour a meal.

'Well, if it isn't the Dandy Highwayman,' she slurred, reaching into her bag to find her keys. 'How did you get here so quickly? Did the girlfriend not want you?'

'She's out for the count. Don't you worry about that. Did you not save me a wee chip, darlin'?' Tommy smirked, taking a drag from the cigarette held between his thumb and forefinger. His lips made a tiny circle at the corner of his mouth to blow the smoke out. It left his mouth in a thin straight line, hung around for a second, and then dissipated.

Maureen nodded toward the chip paper she had just thrown down the close as she walked towards him.

'There might be one left in the paper if you want it.' She retrieved her door key from her bag. Tommy leaned in closely to the side of her face, close enough for Maureen to feel his hot smoky breath on her cheek. She put the key in the top lock and turned to look at him. He noticed her eye make-up had slid down her face and her lipstick was gone; worn off by chip salt and vodka. She shivered as he looked at her, moving from her face to the purple Lycra dress that clung to her curves.

'Were the chips good, then?' he asked, putting a finger under her chin to turn her head upwards towards his face.

'Aye...they were...all right.' Maureen said.

'I can smell the vinegar.' He moved in closer to her face and kissed her forcefully. The door opened and they staggered down the hallway, pausing only for Tommy to kick the door closed.


Frank. Frank, wake up, son. It's twenty to four. He felt June's cold fingers tap lightly on his shoulder and his eyes opened wide. He steadied himself to see June point towards his socks on the floor.

'Yes, dear,' he smiled at her. Reluctantly, he got up and collected each sock. 'Sorry. I'm away up

now,' he said, 'Will you be here when I wake up?'
She smiled softly and ushered him up to bed.

Jackie rolled over to see Tommy's clock flashing
03:44 beside the empty side of the bed. Fully
clothed and still feeling slightly drunk, she looked
around for Tommy, then clutched the sheet tightly.

'Her,' she muttered, through her teeth.

With a low moan she sprung out of bed, clutching
her stomach and ran to the bathroom, knocking
over Tommy's *Denim* aftershave on the way. She
threw up immediately and violently into the toilet,
retching repeatedly. She was shocked at the pain of
the cramp in her stomach. She flushed the toilet
and examined her face in the mirror. *I'm never sick
on drink*, she thought, patting down her bob that
was flattened back against one side of her head.
*Phil Oakey, eat your heart out.*

Her eyes were dry and red. Her cheeks were
blotchy. She cupped some water into her hand to
drink. As soon as the water touched her lips, she
was over the toilet again, gripping the sides.

The gap in the curtains woke Frank before he
wanted to be awake. He looked to the empty side of
the bed and stroked it. Sitting up, his feet felt
around the floor for his slippers, but he couldn't

find them.

'Jackie,' he shouted. 'Jackie? Oh, my head!'

Giving up on the slippers, he walked out of his bedroom door and knocked on Jackie's door.

'Jackie,' he called again, then opened the door cautiously and peeked in. The bed was made neatly, cushions arranged around the pillows and Brown Bear's button eye staring back at him. He stared back at Brown Bear for a second, then closed the door.

'She'll be home in a minute, I'm sure. I'll make tea,' he thought as he wandered down to the kitchen. He opened the fridge door and looked inside, then shut it again. In the reflection of the stainless steel kettle, he noticed two strands of his hair standing up on end. They were normally combed over the top of his bald bit but now they stood to attention. Delighted they were still there, he saluted the two strands reflected in the kettle, then smoothed them down.

He went through to the living room and sat in his chair, clicking on the top button of the TV with the walking stick. Some children dressed in chef hats were cooking something unidentifiable in a kitchen, directed by a posh-looking woman. Frank thought of June, she loved these programmes when she was alive. She watched them intently, sometimes while they ate their dinner off their knees together. She never cooked anything she saw on the TV. Frank hated cooking programmes, but he watched them anyway. He was starving, but not for a 'baked moussaka', whatever that was.

'One of your programmes is on,' he said to the photo of June and motioned to the TV.

The phone rang.

'Is that somebody else copped it now?' he said to the photo as he reluctantly got up to answer it.

'Hello, can I speak to the owner of the house?'

'Who is it?'

'This is Starstore double-glazing. Have you heard of us at all?'

'Do you know what day it is, hen?'

'Yes, sorry to bother you -'

'Aye that's right. It's Saturday. And I've not even had my cup of tea. Have you had a cup of tea?'

'I've had a wee coffee.'

'A wee coffee? That's nice. I've always been a tea man, myself. I leave the bag in. I like it strong.'

'Are you satisfied with your windows and doors?'

'Very satisfied, hen. Delighted with my windows and doors. How are your windows and doors?'

'Er -'

'Enjoy your coffee now. Bye!' Frank walked into the living room and sat back down. He took a sip of tea. 'Ach!' He got up and went into the kitchen and poured the cold tea down the sink. The phone rang again as he was stirring a fresh cup.

'Oh, come on, for buck's sake!' He tiptoed his way over the lino, but there was no avoiding the sugar he'd spilled the night before, and it crept in between his toes. He had forgotten to use the tea towels.

'Now I told you I was - oh Jackie! Yes, it is me, Jackie...aye and about time. Where are you...? Don't tell me...Well, it's time you were home...Well, I told you to slow down on that vodka, it's lethal stuff, hen. You'd be better off with a half lager or somethi...Well, what time will that be...?' Frank twisted his foot from side to side, trying to get rid of sugar on the carpet. 'Aye, 'cos I'm starving. That's me just getting my tea now. Bring sausages n' eggs as well. That fridge is empty and ma feet are covered in sugar, have you seen my slippers... Jackie, you there? Jackie?'

He put the phone down, then turned quickly to go back to the living room, catching his toe on the doorframe. He drew in a deep, sharp breath.

'Oh...' he sucked, 'Oh, ma toe...ma toe ma toe ma toe...' He hopped through into the living room to his chair. 'Oh, ma toe ma toe ma toe...' He took a cushion from behind his back, pulled over the coffee table and put his foot on it. His toe looked red. He touched it, then sucked in a breath again. He sat back in the chair and tried to watch the children dressed as chefs serve up the dish of baked moussaka to the posh woman. He leaned forward every now and then to touch his toe, sucking in at the pain. 'Where are you when I need you?' he said to the photograph. 'And hurry up, Jackie!'

Tommy closed Maureen's bedroom door quietly and walked through the living room to her front door. Pulling it behind him, he lit up a Rothman's, took a deep drag and strode off down the close. The thin milky stripe trailed behind him in the air.

The handle of the shopping bag cut into Jackie's swollen fingers as she rested it down on the step to put the key in her front door.

'I'm in here,' shouted Frank. Jackie walked in and saw Frank with his foot up on the table.

'What happened?' she puffed, as she laid the bag on the kitchen worktop, then returned to examine her dad's foot.

'Banged ma toe on the door. Nearly broke it ... don't touch it, ah -'

'Sorry, Dad. Will I make you a wee tea?'

'Yes. And put the pan on, I'm starving. Nothing since yesterday. Stomach thinks ma throat's been cut.'

'What's all this sugar all over the floor?'

'Aye, that as well... I had a wee accident.' Frank settled back in his chair, moving a cushion to position himself more comfortably. Jackie clattered around in the kitchen slamming cupboard doors, cracking eggs into a pan and sweeping up sugar.

'That's the breakfast on!' he said to the picture of June, rubbing his hands.

'What's that, Dad?' Jackie peered around the door, brush in hand.

'Nothing, hen, just the telly. Did you get rolls?'

'Aye, I got rolls.' Jackie went to check the eggs. She rubbed at the pain in her head and poured herself a glass of water from the tap.

'She's the one that's gallivanting to all hours, not me. She should be at home with me instead of having nights at...well...wherever she goes. I bet you wherever she goes is a dirty hole as well. Although the amount of women he has round there, it should be spotless.' Frank finished the tea in the cup. 'And here's me, an old man. With a sore toe. A broken toe. My toe's maybe broke, you know, June.'

'Dad,' Jackie tapped Frank's shoulder.

'Oh, hen, you gave me a fright!'

'You're scaring me.'

'How's that, hen?' Frank took the tray from

Jackie's hands onto his knee.

'Dad, you've got to stop it.' Jackie took her roll and tea from the tray.

'Stop what?' Frank's mouth was full of sausage. He cut another piece off as he chewed.

'Talking to her. She's gone, Dad.' Jackie stood over him, looking into his eyes, then looking at the picture on the mantelpiece. Frank paused, then continued eating. Jackie flopped down onto the couch and took a bite of her roll, then put it back down on the plate and pushed it away. Frank cleared his plate of food, then held the tray up.

'Good lassie,' he smiled as she stood up to take the empty plate and tray. 'Are you feeling all right, hen? You've not ate much,' he said, swapping the tray for her roll and taking a bite out of it.

'I had something earlier.' Jackie took the tray into the kitchen and put it down. She felt a bit light-headed and steadied herself against the counter. She searched around the bottom of the shopping bag until she found what she was looking for - a pregnancy test.

# A BETTER FATHER

Jackie had given herself a few days to deal with the fact that she was expecting a baby. Half of those days had been spent stewing and questioning Tommy over his absence the other night. Between the two thoughts, her stomach felt like a washing machine on spin.

He claimed he went out to an all-night party at a friend's, and that she shouldn't fill her head with nonsense that wasn't true. He offered one of the guys from the betting shop as an alibi, but deep down she knew already, and didn't want to think about what the truth was.

She had taken several tests, all positive, and been to the doctor.

'That's a positive pregnancy!' the out of town GP smiled as she told her.

There was no escaping it. She knew Tommy would explode, so she decided to tell her dad first, that she was pregnant and wanted to keep the baby. There was no way she could get rid of it. She hoped for the best, and, as her dad's happiest mood was around dinnertime, she told him then.

Frank sat still in his chair, as Jackie waited for an

answer. He placed his fork gently onto the plate with a little 'clink' and arranged it in a straight line next to three uneaten boiled potatoes and a slice of poached haddock in milk, his favourite. He stared at the warm fish, unable to eat it, the word 'pregnant' stuck in his throat like a stone. He'd had the same sort of reaction when he got the news that June was dying. The words unable to be swallowed, or vomited, just held there, hard, like a lift stuck between two floors.

Now she was one of those girls... and unmarried. Maybe Fletcher attacked her? Conflicting thoughts and images flew around his brain forwards, backwards, twisting. *But! She's Jackie...my girl... the girl that I bought bon bons for and she'd give me one from the white packet, then we'd go to the park and spin on the roundabout. Who is Jackie? Where is that Jackie that I tickled on my knee? I've only just met this guy Tommy!*

Jackie sat quietly, searching his face, desperate for a glimpse into his thoughts. She could see disappointment, shock and shame cloud his eyes. She'd never wanted to hurt her dad, this just happened. She felt stupid.

'Shameful! I'm pure ashamed!' her mum would say, if she was here.

'Don't think less of me, Dad, please don't ...' The

words burst out of her. 'I'm still me.' She twisted the end of her cardigan around her index finger and back again. She knew that a part of his love for her, the little girl part, might be gone forever and right now, she just wanted to leap into his arms and be cuddled and carried.

Frank took the tray off his knee and put it onto the floor. He got up and walked out of the room to the front door. He opened it wide to the street, and breathed in the late afternoon cold air. He could see his breath. He stopped in the middle of the small front garden with his hands deep in his pockets, looking out at the view of the Town Clock. Jackie stood behind him at the door.

'I'm sorry, Dad. Dad, I'm so sorry,' she wept, walking towards him. 'Please, Dad, say you still love me, Dad, please.' She tried to put her arms around his neck. He kept his hands in his pockets as she buried her sobbing face deep into his jumper. Reluctantly, his arms folded her into him.

'Of course I do,' he replied. Frank felt like he was sinking down into the grass as the garden spun around him. He fished in his pocket for a tissue. 'Here, blow.'

Jackie took the tissue, wiped her eyes and blew her nose. He put his hands on her shoulders and looked into her eyes.

'Are you keeping it?' he asked.

'Aye, I've used it.' She put the tissue in her pocket and sniffed.

'I meant the baby,' Frank tutted.

'I won't get rid of it. I can't do that...No way.' She searched for the tissue and blew her nose again. 'Anyway ...' she blew again. 'He'll stand by me.'

'It's Fletcher's?' he asked, gently. She nodded. 'And that's what he said? He said those words - "I'll stand by you"?'

Jackie shrugged. 'Well, not those exact words, I mean, I haven't really told him yet...' Frank grimaced. Jackie raised her eyebrows in response, 'He will, Dad! He will. We've talked about this,' she lied. 'He will.'

'How far gone are you?'

'Thirteen weeks. It's due in September.'

An old lady walked by. The wheels of her tartan shopping trolley stopped squeaking for a few seconds as she leaned in to peer over the gate.

Frank sighed.

'Let's go in,' he said, putting a hand on Jackie's back. The front door closed behind them and the trolley wheels began squeaking again. Jackie excused herself to go upstairs to the toilet. Frank walked slowly into the living room and sat down on the couch, a place he never usually sat. He rubbed one hand on the flat, square arm. June was sitting in the other chair.

'What now?' he asked her. He swallowed hard. 'What am I supposed to do now?' A single tear traced the long deep laughter line of his right cheek. June shook her head and patted down her knee, wiping away invisible crumbs. 'Will he stand by her? How am I going to get him to stand by her? Do we want him to stand by her?'

They sat in silence for a few minutes, then Frank sniffed, stood up and adjusted his belt to fit in a tighter hole, then decided it was fine in the belt hole it was already in.

'Right then,' he announced, and went upstairs to knock on the bathroom door. 'Jackie. You okay, hen?'

'I'm okay. Are you okay?'

'Aye. I'm going out for a wee walk.'

'Okay. I'm just going to have a quick bath, Dad.'

'Right you are. I won't be long now.'

'Where are you going?'

'Nowhere... Just a walk.'

'Oh, okay, see you in a wee while.' He walked away from the door, paused, and then went back.

'Listen, everything is going to be all right... okay?' The words struggled to leave his throat.

'Okay.' Jackie sat down on the toilet seat.

Hearing her dad go down the stairs, she looked down at her little belly and put a hand on it.

'There. We'll be all right,' she whispered. 'Your Granda said it.' Hearing the back door slam, she turned both taps on full. The rush of water muffled her wails and she cried freely; the first time since the death of her mother.

Frank began the fifteen-minute walk to the bookies where Tommy Fletcher worked. He wished now more than ever that June was here to talk him down, to walk beside him. He was up too high and the rage pumped through the veins of his old body, making it feel twenty again. His hands made fists as he stomped down the road. He looked around for June. He thought that she'd want Fletcher to stand by Jackie. He needed to get Fletcher in line, and that's exactly what he was going to do. He couldn't make him be faithful, but he was damn sure that the lad would not shirk his duties as a father.

'For God's sake, Jackie, why him? Of all the guys round here, why him?' he said to the pavement, kicking a stone into the gutter, forgetting about his sore toe. 'What kind of dad will he make?' he wondered, visualising Jackie surrounded by nappies and Fletcher nowhere to be seen. He turned the corner to see the sign of his shop and his eyes bore into the Fletcher's sign.

'Enough!' he seethed.

Pushing the door open to Fletcher's bookmakers, he noticed the little bell ring. Expecting the shop to be empty, he was caught off guard as two men were in making a bet. Both wore shell suits and he could hear them talking and laughing with Tommy. Frank took a betting slip and small blue pen and stood by the window.

'You might as well walk out now, lads! You won't be seeing any winners with that old knacker! I've seen your mammy run faster for a cone off the ice cream van.'

'Now you hold your own horses there, Tommy. Joey's Dream can take this.'

'At fifty to one?' Tommy Fletcher's hollow laugh bellowed; he had a slightly crazed look in his eyes.

'They're off!' one of the men pointed. 'C'mon, Joey's Dream! C'mon, son!'

'Here he comes!' shouted the smaller man. 'He's coming round, he's coming! He's going to take it, I can feel it, come on, Joey's Dream! Come on now, Come on, Joey's Dream! COME ON, JOEY'S DREAM!' Both men shouted at the small TV screen on the wall. They began jumping up and down as Joey's Dream overtook horse after horse, picking up pace and galloping on ahead. Frank watched the colour drain from Tommy's face as, mouth agape, he stood up, his wheelie chair gently rolling away from the back of his knees.

'NAW!' he shouted. 'NAW! PADDIE'S CROSS! PADDIE'S CROSS!' Tommy pointed at the screen, his cheeks now reddening. 'PADDIE'S CROSS MAKES YE LOSS! PADDIE'S CROSS!' he screamed, his voice higher than a dog yelp.

'Paddie cannae help ye now, Tommy, son!' The two men laughed and clasped each other's shoulders.

'Joey's Dream is a dead cert!' the taller man started shouting again. 'He's yompin' it!'

'Here he comes! Look at that! How many furlongs is that? He's a bullet!' The larger man had the smaller man's shoulder in a tight grip.

'Unstoppable!' said the smaller man.

'Oh, my God, look at that! Here he's coming. HERE HE'S COMING. HE'S GONNIE DO IT! HE'S GONNIE WIN. HE'S WON IT! EYYYYYY!' Both men danced around in a circle doing a doe-see-doe as they watch the horse slow its gallop to a canter, the other horses struggling for second place.

Tommy bit his lip, and closed his eyes. Frank's fingers unclenched from their fists, relaxing his grip on the tiny pen.

Tommy reluctantly counted out £200.

'Ten, twenty, thirty, forty, fifty...'

The two men watched intently as the notes flip-flapped.

'And the stake!' one of them said. 'Don't forget the stake!'

'Here's your stake.'

'Thank you! Maybe see you tomorrow, Tommy, if you're lucky!'

'Aye, be lucky, Tommy!' The two men laughed their way out of the bookies.

Tommy rested his head in his hands, brushed them down his face, then noticed Frank.

'Oh, it's you. We're shut.' He turned off the TV with a remote control.

Frank stared.

'What do you want?' he asked Frank.

Frank couldn't find any words.

'What is it...?'

'Nothing.' Frank said, putting the pen and slip down on the side. He walked out of the bookies and headed home. His toe was feeling a little bit better.

Tommy shook his head at Frank's strange behaviour and gathered himself to clean up. 'Joey's nightmare,' he muttered, as he walked around the shop. About to crumple up the slip that Frank had left, he noticed something strange about the handwriting:

4.55 - Airdrie

Jackie's pregnant.

He had never heard of that horse – and there was no racetrack in Airdrie.

# TEABAGS

After Jackie moved in with Tommy, Frank had to fend for himself. He was starving. He'd had nothing but a salted tomato and a cup of tea since two o'clock and it was now half past six. Giving up on Jackie coming round with food again, he opened the back door to go to the corner shop for a cold pie and nearly tripped over the glorious sight of a casserole dish wrapped in a Linlithgow tea towel. He picked it up and had a good sniff; a stew from Mrs Morrisson down the road.

'You absolute dancer!' he exclaimed.

Jackie was heavily pregnant and only came around when she could manage the journey. With that in mind, Frank relished any casseroles, stews, sandwiches and iced buns from lonely old neighbour widows.

Mrs Morrisson and Frank were only on a 'Hello' basis. He'd first noticed her overly sympathetic looks and tut noises on the return bus from Fine Fare one day. She was a few years older than him, dyed-ash-blonde curly hair and a pink overcoat, which she never zipped up. It struggled to meet the middle and she had a habit of pulling the two open flaps of the jacket across when she wanted to make a serious point. In his own strange way, Frank was grateful that she was one of those old ladies that liked to have somebody to feed, and he was happy to take her food, but that was all.

After heating the casserole in the oven, Frank sat it down on a tray, and ate it straight from the dish with a spoon in front of the news. The reporter with the big teeth was doing a feature on London buses. Frank had never been to London and had no intention of doing so after hearing that John Dunn paid £1.90 for a bowl of minestrone soup in a pub and they never gave him any bread.

*Coronation Street* came on and the familiar music welcomed his warm memories of June again.

'Change it, Frank, hurry up, my programme's on. It's so and so's wedding,' she'd say. She never warmed to *Emmerdale Farm* on STV but she watched it anyway so that she could talk to her friends about how terrible it was.

'Och, it was on but I wasn't watching it,' she'd say, 'I cannot stick that posh couple on it.' He was never a fan of soaps, and moaned when she put it on, but if it came on now, he liked to see the familiarity of the cobbles and the cat and the Rovers Return, maybe see if Hilda Ogden would give him a laugh.

# Frank

He was always pleased when something triggered a little memory of June, something he could enjoy for a minute or two. Something he'd forgotten that would occupy his time. Mopping up the last spoon of gravy, he turned off the TV, and put the unwashed casserole dish onto the back step. He threw the spoon in the sink. He put on his bunnet and jacket and headed out to The Black Dog for a quiet pint. Sometimes it was just too hard to stay in.

Frank liked to go to The Black Dog occasionally on a Thursday. It wasn't as good as the Working Men's Club but there was generally something on, either a quiz or bingo or an entertainer and it was only down the road. This week, the small local was busy as local celebrity Jimmy Diamond was playing his keyboard. He didn't mind a bit of Jimmy Diamond, but he didn't much like his Elvis suits. Frank ordered a pint and stood at the bar keeping his jacket on. He had a look around and gave a few nods, and a woman that June knew - Bessie Smith - came to the bar to get drinks. Jackie was best friends with her daughter, Viv. Frank used to play dominoes with her husband years ago and remembered he had a bad leg.

'Hiya, Frank, how's it goin' with you?'

'How do, Bessie. How's his leg?'

'Aye, still giving him jip. I had to leave him in

front of the telly with a can. Ah cannae miss Jimmy Diamond, Frank.'

Jimmy Diamond finished *Cracklin' Rosie* and Bessie left the bar abruptly to applaud him. She squeezed onto the small space of carpet between tables to dance to *Viva Las Vegas*. Soon after, many people started to squeeze onto the small dance floor. The pub got crowded and the bar was heaving. Frank decided he wasn't in the mood tonight but couldn't fathom why. Usually, the drink worked a treat but not tonight. He finished his pint anyway, and walked the long way home.

Waking up fresher than he'd anticipated, he had a shave and decided it was time to go to Fine Fare and get some provisions of his own. He walked down to get the bus, which arrived just as he got to the bus stop. He paid and sat down at the window. Looking around at the other passengers, he noticed how everybody seemed older. Even the ones he thought were 'young' were now in their forties, with jogging trousers and downtrodden faces. Those weans he knew now had their own weans; all dummies and dirty smiles. The bus teemed with weans, beside him, behind him, all screaming for a biscuit.

*Oh God, this will be Jackie soon*, he thought.

*That low life only took her in because she's pregnant. Still, it's the right thing.* He looked out of the window.

The bus stopped and Mrs Morrisson got on. Panicking, Frank turned his head right around to look behind himself as if he'd seen something amazing out of the window behind the bus.

'How did you enjoy the casserole, Frank?' She sat down on the empty seat beside him, resting her bag on her knee.

'Oh, hello, Mrs! Was that casserole from you? I didn't recognise the tea towel...If I'd known, I would've...'

'Of course it was me! You know my son lives in Linlithgow, I've told you that before.' They sat in silence, both staring directly ahead. 'He got me that tea towel.'

Frank knew if he was to receive more casseroles, he'd better act grateful. He lowered his voice to a whisper and leaned in.

'That was nice of you, though, thanks. I was just so glad to have a good meal inside me. I've not eaten so well since our Jackie up and left me on my own in that house.'

'Oh, did she move in with the bookie? How is she keeping? You'll need help when the baby comes.'

'She did. She's fine. She still visits, but it's not

easy with our June being gone, God rest her soul.'

'Well...Yes, I suppose. I remember when our John died. I was -'

'Oh jings, that's my stop, Mrs. I'll see you soon... You take care now!' Frank pushed past her, trying not to let his bum touch her bag, and clumsily trundled off the bus. He walked straight into Father Cleary from St Mary's, who was eating an apple.

'Oh, hello, Father! Lovely day. See you at Mass!'

'Yes, Frank, it would be nice to have you back...' The priest wanted to continue the conversation, but Frank was already down the road going the other way. He turned into the main street, and waved to the priest behind him.

'Right, what is it that we need again, did you say?' June smiled sweetly. 'Did you say teabags?' Frank stood at the entrance. A shopper looked at him and wondered who he was talking to. 'A priest! Eating an apple! In the street! Have you ever seen the likes of it, would you tell me now...?' he asked June.

Frank didn't think he wanted enough food for a trolley, but took one as June motioned for him to. He didn't want too much to carry.

'I should have one of them,' he said to June, pointing to an electric wheelchair with a basket attached to the front. 'I'm getting that on the NHS if they say my toe's broken.'

Your toe's not broken. You wouldn't be able to walk, you eejit, he heard. They walked towards the loose potatoes.

'I'm telling you, that was some crack it took.' Frank put a few potatoes in a bag, not sure of how many to put in. June motioned for him to put more in, then held her hand up for him to stop. Another wheelchair whizzed past with a full shopping basket.

'Hey – there's another one – I told you! They give them out like sweeties. Half the folk in they things don't need them. Some of them go faster than the one-four-seven –'

'Afternoon again, Frank,' said Father Cleary.

'Oh, hello, Father...Hello again.' Frank snatched a glance to his left, June wasn't there. He looked back at the priest, patted a hand flat on his chest and bowed slightly, feeling guilty because he'd run off and left him before.

'Haven't seen you at Mass in a while, since June passed, God rest her soul.' The priest made the Sign of the Cross and looked up at the roof, then back to Frank. 'How are you keeping?' he asked, looking over his glasses.

'Oh, you know, Father, struggling on. Like the good soldier!' Frank fiddled with potatoes, putting more and more into the bag.

'That's a lot of potatoes.' Father Cleary nodded to the full bag.

Frank put a few back, then put the bag in the trolley. The priest motioned for Frank to follow him down the chilled aisle. He felt awkward as their trolleys rolled side by side.

'You should pop in to the parish house, Frank. Have a cup of tea. To tell you the truth, I could use you to help with collections, if you'd like to? It's been very busy with the feast days. An extra pair of hands is always welcome. It's good to keep ourselves busy in times like these.'

'Well, I've been busy...with Jackie, you know, she needs me for the shopping and so on.'

'Oh, she still visits, that's nice. I believe the Fletcher fellow she's with is not a church goer?' Frank shrugged. 'Are they marrying?'

'Not as I believe, Father. Sorry about that.'

'I see. Not at all, not at all, Frank. It is the way of the young these days. It's not the Lord's way...but I do wish Jackie good health. When is the baby due?'

'Next month.'

'Maybe I can pop over to your house one day after the baby comes?'

'Aye, that'd be fine. Well, if you're coming, I'd better go and get some Fondant Fancies and get the Hoover out!' Frank laughed at his own joke but the priest just smiled gently.

'No need for that, now,' said Father Cleary. 'A rich tea will do! Or a custard cream. I'm partial to those.' He had a stare that made Frank feel like he needed to go to confession. 'Phone the parish house to arrange a suitable time, Frank. Number's on the bulletin, I'm sure you have a copy. God bless, now.'

He gave a little bow and Frank bowed back, then walked away. Father Cleary watched Frank as he turned down the aisle. He followed him until he was far enough away at the cheeses and listened to him mutter to himself about whether it's red cheese or yellow cheese. He seemed to be speaking to the left side of the trolley. 'It's you that likes the yellow. I like the red.' The priest watched intently, then sighed as he put some double cream in the trolley, next to a rhubarb pie.

'I haven't seen my dad in a few days. Fancy going to see him with me?' said Jackie, wiping down the Formica table behind the couch in Tommy's flat. Tommy was reading the paper and picking his teeth. His feet rested on the other edge of the couch. He kept his shoes on, even though he'd been home for an hour.

'I've got work. You go.'

'Well, I struggle with the journey now, a bit.'

Jackie looked at the side of Tommy's face, hoping for an answer, hoping he'd say, 'Just get a taxi, here's the money,' or 'I'll take you, darlin',' or anything. She wanted him to say anything at all, but he seemed so distracted since she moved in. She had been sick and in bed with the pregnancy and struggled with the flights of stairs up and down to the flat. Alone much of the time inside, she had developed a compulsion to clean, and would often seek out corners of cupboards or tops of doorframes that had never seen a duster.

Some nights, Tommy never returned from work, and she never asked why, preferring to think he was busy stocktaking at the bookies, or whatever it was he said they did there. Maybe he went for a pint, but she could never smell lager on his breath. He had sworn that it was over with that Maureen one, that it was only one time, just a drunken kiss, never meant anything. She believed him, as it was convenient to do so. She busied herself cleaning the legs of the table, looking at the flat pack baby crib, still in the MFI box.

'Maybe my dad could come here?' she asked, carefully, hoping Tommy was in the right mood.

'Whatever...' he offered, dismissively. As far as Jackie was concerned, that was the green light to make a phone call.

'Great! I'll go and phone him now! Thanks, Tommy!' She kissed his head and he let out a moan about watching his hair and waved her away. She didn't care, she was too happy that her dad was coming for lunch, and went to the hall to use the phone. She returned to the living room a few minutes later.

'He'll be here on Sunday,' she smiled at Tommy, clasping her hands to her chest. 'I might ask Viv as well, if that's okay with you? I haven't seen her for ages either...'

Tommy turned the page of his paper. 'Whatever,' he said, and continued to read.

'Right then!' Jackie announced to the gleaming flat. 'A wee cuppa tea, I think.'

'You're such an old woman,' said Tommy. Jackie stayed silent. She filled the kettle and took two mugs out of the cupboard.

# SUNDAY LUNCH

Frank took the short cut off the bus to the new scheme where Tommy lived. He climbed two flights of stairs to Tommy's flat and the strong smell of bleach caught his throat.

The quiet old woman from across the landing was out scrubbing on her hands and knees, a heavy bucket of suds beside her. With sleeves rolled up tight to the shoulder, her slackened skin flapped back and forth like a sail on windy water. She dug the brush into the grey stone, cleaning with brute force, bleach and rage.

'Hello, Mrs!' smiled Frank. She paused and looked up.

'There's a rota for cleaning this close, you know!' She pointed her brush to Tommy's door. Her gnarled fingers were clamped around the wood like old tree roots. 'It's supposed to be his turn! And here I am doing it for him, again. The bloody liberty!' She resumed scratching the brush on the ground. 'If it wasn't for that poor girl in there, I wouldn't be doing it! I can tell you that, right now.'

She continued scrubbing. Frank tiptoed around the soapy puddle onto the lighter grey stone part of the landing and rang the bell of Flat 16, which made an elongated 'ding-dong' noise, and footsteps approached the door from the other side.

It was her bump that he saw first, a great big hard belly of baby reaching right round in front of her like a whale's nose. With one hand supporting her back, she stretched out the other to welcome him into a cuddle. Her familiar scent of youth replaced the bleach in his nostrils and he breathed it in gratefully. He kissed her forehead and smiled, looking for his welcome from her beautiful green eyes. She beamed her greatest grin but her eyes were as ringed as Saturn.

'You look exhausted, hen.'

'I'm fine, Dad, come in. Hello, Mrs... and thanks, again...' The lady on the landing nodded and ushered Jackie to go in. 'I'm having a bit of trouble sleeping,' said Jackie as she closed the door, 'It's hard to get comfy with a big lump.'

'Now, you shouldn't talk about Tommy like that!' he whispered, mischievously. They both laughed as she led him down the hall into the lounge.

'Tommy! My dad's here!' she announced. Frank smiled.

'What's the big joke?' asked Tommy from behind a newspaper.

'Ah, nothing. How are things with you, Tommy?'

Pleased with his joke at the door, Frank was determined to make the effort to have a nice afternoon. He tried to swallow down his resentment towards Tommy and make the best of the day. Tommy peeked over his newspaper and nodded.

'Fine,' he offered, 'Mister McNeill.' He took no notice of whether Frank answered.

'Now, now, call me Frank, we're practically family here!' He tried to cover the tension with a laugh, but it was hollow. *I'm sure the horses are much more interesting than your girlfriend's dad*, thought Frank. It ached him to know that this was the way things were now, and Tommy was the man of this house, the father of the baby.

Tommy occupied the entire couch, so Frank took a hard seat by the small folding table. On it sat a picture of June, Frank and Jackie as a baby on the beach in Arbroath. *Different days then*...he thought, then shrugged, *I looked good in my trunks*. He picked up the frame to take a closer look at his chest, and absentmindedly sucked his stomach in.

'What time are we eating?' Tommy shouted through to the kitchen, as he flipped the paper over to re-read the front page.

'Half an hour. Just waiting for Viv,' Jackie shouted back through kitchen noises. Frank felt relieved. Jackie came back through with two cans of beer. 'It's still okay if Viv comes, isn't it, Tommy?'

'I already said yes, didn't I? It's a bit late to start asking me again now, isn't it?' sniped Tommy, rushing the Tennent's can to his mouth.

The doorbell rang.

'That'll be her.' Jackie hobbled to the door, her penguin feet pointed in opposite directions.

'You look massive!' squealed Viv, eyes huge and mouth wide.

'I know!' Jackie laughed, 'not long now!'

Viv put her light brown fake leather fringed bag down at the side of the couch. She jangled with bangles and every finger had a ring. Frank had never seen her with the same bag twice, each one selected to match her outfit. Her make-up was like something off the TV, red lipstick pencilled on the liner first around the edges, then coloured in expertly, never going over the tips of the pointed 'M' drawn on the top lip. Jackie said she had more lipsticks than Boots. Viv had taken a job with Avon selling make-up door to door and at parties, and seemed to be never short of a few pounds. Today she wore a horizontal striped top, stone washed jeans and braces, and had added a beauty spot beside her right eye. She had the same style as Jackie before she got pregnant, the only difference being the hair and the amount of make-up; Viv's hair was backcombed high with hairspray while Jackie's brown bob cupped her cheeks like chocolate on a Malteser.

'Here's a wee thing for the baby.' Jackie opened a Mothercare bag to find a tiny lemon babygro with white poppers all down the front and a teddy on the chest pocket.

'Aww, that's gorgeous. I love it, Viv! Thanks, hen.' She gave Viv a hug.

'Tommy, look! It's dead cute, isn't it, Dad?'

'Aye, that's lovely, hen,' Frank said. 'I'm sure you had one like that when you were a wean...' he continued, 'It wouldn't fit you now though!'

He hid his smile behind his can, then the three erupted in laughter as Viv patted Jackie's bump. The laughter released a closeness between them that warmed the air. For just a flash, Frank thought he saw June sitting on the edge of the couch to the right of Tommy, joining in and pointing. Tommy shivered and lit a cigarette.

Jackie and Viv retreated to the kitchen to check on the chicken. Frank felt happy that Viv was there. He had always been fond of Viv and had known her since she was a child. A permanent figure on their living room carpet after school, Viv would lie on the floor beside Jackie, chins in their hands, eating crisps and watching *Top Of The Pops*. Frank remembered them showing off their green tongues after drinking all the lime Alpine. June would watch them from the couch, knitting and smiling.

They came back in from the kitchen.

'I was just remembering the time you had green tongues from the Alpine man's limeade!' said Frank, looking for another laugh.

'I remember that!' said Viv. 'God, I was always in your house.'

'Tell me about it. There was never anything in that fridge!' he laughed. 'There's more in the fridge now, and last I looked, that was just a tomato-'

'How long till the dinner, Jackie, for God's sake?' Tommy interrupted, slicing through Frank's punchline.

'I'll just check again.' Jackie held her back as she returned to the kitchen, Viv following her closely with offers of help. Frank was left in the quiet with Tommy. Tommy crushed his can, and threw it in the waste paper basket by the fire.

'Bring us in another can,' he shouted towards the kitchen. 'You want another can?' he asked Frank.

'Aye, okay, if that's okay, I mean, if there's enough.'

'Bring your dad another can as well!' he shouted back to the kitchen, 'Aye, there's enough,' he said, turning towards Frank, 'There's always plenty of beer in this house, which is lucky, isn't it, as you didn't bother to bring any.' Panic rose within Frank. Was he supposed to bring beer? On a Sunday? June would have known this. He tried to placate Tommy.

'I thought it was just a -'

'Just forget it,' Tommy spat.

Frank looked down at his shoes. Viv returned with two cans.

'Here you go, boys, enjoy.' She handed them both a can each.

'If you're sure?' Frank offered the can to Tommy.

'I said, just forget it, didn't I? Drink your drink.'

'It's ready!' announced Jackie. She emerged from the kitchen with a small, perfectly cooked roast chicken resting on the top of her pregnant belly, beads of perspiration on her forehead, and a triumphant smile.

'I've never cooked a chicken before!'

'Your mum would be proud of you!' smiled Viv.

'Here's hoping we all don't die,' Tommy muttered, putting out a cigarette.

They sat around the Formica table on three-legged stools. Jackie plugged in an electric knife to carve the chicken.

'Oh, fancy!' said Viv, 'Posh that, in't it, Frank?'

Jackie smiled, happy that someone noticed her

new knife. 'I collected coupons from the paper.' Everybody watched the knife carve through the chicken, making a loud sound like a hedge cutter.

Frank held his plate up for some chicken. Tommy already had his on his plate. Satisfied that he had a good bit of white and brown meat with all the vegetables and gravy, Frank squeezed half a potato onto his fork with a chunk of the leg.

'This is lovely, hen,' he offered, being careful not to irritate Tommy. Frank's knife and fork clinked unusually loudly. He decided to stay quiet and wait for somebody else to talk.

'It's Mum's anniversary this Wednesday, Dad.'

'I know.'

'I can't believe it's been a year.'

'Neither can I.'

'Are you going to the grave?'

'Oh, yes, hen, I am. I wouldn't miss it.'

'I'll meet you there,' said Jackie.

'You should take a taxi, Jackie,' said Viv, pointing to Jackie's bump. 'I'll give you the mo-'

'No need. I'll be fine, Viv, honest.' She patted Viv's hand, appreciating her offer. Viv knew she couldn't afford a taxi and it was two buses to the graveyard.

'Smashing this, hen,' said Frank, focusing on the food.

Tommy checked his watch and rubbed the last potato around his plate before shoving the whole thing into his mouth and pushing the plate away.

'Tommy! You ate that quick! Must have been good?' she asked eagerly. 'I hope you've got room for the gateau,' she continued, 'I've just taken it out the freezer!' Jackie could never anticipate Tommy's moods, but his actions made her feel uneasy. A look at his watch usually meant he had to be somewhere.

'No cream cake for me. I'm needed at the bookies.'

'On a Sunday?' Jackie's brow was furrowed. She gathered up empty plates.

'Aye. Paper work. Won't be too long.' Tommy got up, wiped his mouth and brushed past Jackie, briefly kissing her on the head. 'Don't wait up,' he said as he stopped momentarily to check himself in the hall mirror. He pulled down his shirt cuffs and said, 'I've a lot to do. Bye, Vivien. Mr McNeill.'

Jackie avoided her dad's glance, smiled and loudly piled the cutlery on the plates. Viv looked at Frank. He looked back and raised his eyebrows. She shrugged and went into the kitchen to help Jackie wash up.

Frank stayed at the table to wait for the gateau. He thought it better to let the women talk about it. Best he didn't mention Tommy's departure. After all, it wasn't really his business. He looked around the little room and noticed a large brown box propped against the wall.

'What's in the box, hen?'

'Oh, that's the baby's cot. I haven't taken it out of the box yet. It needs to be assembled. Tommy said he'd do it but he's so busy with work at the moment...'

'Does he keep a tool box?'

'I don't know, Dad, maybe in that cupboard, he keeps his stuff like that in there.'

'I'll look,' said Viv, drying her hands and walking to the little door. She bent down and opened it with a stiff click. She could see a few screws, a hammer, a roll of black tape and a box. She reached for the box and opened it to find a birthday card. She opened it and read, *To my big stud, happy birthday, M.* She quickly stuffed the card back into the box and pushed the box back to where it was. She rummaged around near the hammer and found two old screwdrivers tucked in behind it.

*Who's M?* Viv wondered. *Mum? Whose mum calls them a stud? How old is that card? No way. Could it be that Maureen? It might be an old card, though. No point telling Jackie,* she thought, *she might have seen it, it's probably really old, been lying in there for years.*

Tommy had to rush. He couldn't spend another minute in there with Frank's stupid jokes and Jackie's fussing. He felt suffocated. When he told Maureen about the lunch during the week, she told him if he got bored to just come over and she'd have a 'pudding' waiting. Jackie could carry on without him. He was the one that took her in, provided a roof and food and bed for her and the kid. She had her dad and her friend round, what more did she want from him? It was his flat! It was his money that paid for that chicken that her dad so enjoyed. He lit a cigarette and headed towards Maureen's house. He was entitled to his fun, too. Maureen's place wasn't far from the bookies so he was able to take the same route. He was thinking of giving Maureen a job at the bookies. She'd be good with the punters, maybe better than Ginger Terry who couldn't count. Tommy wondered if Maureen was any good with numbers. He headed down the long straight road of small grey terraced houses and took a right turn down the narrow close that led to the door of Number 36.

'Any joy with tools in there, Viv?' Frank was standing above her.

'I found these.' She passed out two screwdrivers of different sizes.

'They'll do,' said Frank. 'Let's get this box open before this wean makes its appearance.' Viv stood up and wiped down her knees. She looked at Jackie who was holding her hands up under her chin and beaming at her dad as he stripped open the cardboard and flung it high over the table onto the couch. Jackie began laughing at her dad's antics.

'You're mental!' she exclaimed.

Frank beamed at her, throwing cardboard here and there and making 'wee!' noises. Viv laughed along. She decided to put the card to the back of her mind, for now.

# A JUNE BIRTHDAY

On Wednesday morning, Frank put on his best tie and headed for the graveyard, picking up some chrysanthemums on the way. On arrival at the gravestone, he was taken aback to see that the wind had blown the steel vase with the holes over, and dead flowers were scattered around the edges of the plot. He picked up each dead flower and laid them to one side, before he inserted the fresh flowers carefully into each hole. The vase still had some water in the bottom, enough to keep the flowers alive until the rain came on again.

He looked around the graveyard for her, thinking he might see her today, but no sign. He hadn't seen her since he went to Tommy's flat on Sunday, and that was only briefly. It wasn't long enough, and she wasn't there when he got home on Sunday night either. He indulged himself in a happy memory as he stared at the new grass poking through the earth. He was back in the Club with June on a Friday night, looking fantastic, the talk of the town, on top of the world, dancing the night away. But the memory was soiled as soon as she hit the vodka.

'I'm just going to have a couple the night,' she'd

say. She'd get too drunk to dance, and those nights would end with him pouring her into a taxi in her ripped tights, which the next day she'd claim were not worth the money she'd paid for them.

*No! no!* he thought, *I want this memory to be happy; I don't want to go here.* A strong image of her hospital bed was now in his head. She lay there, asleep, in a pale pink cotton nightgown. Still pretty on the outside; her looks never reflected what was going on inside; a useless liver that could no longer repair itself; and no hope of a donor. Cirrhosis. What an ugly word.

Frank's thoughts were interrupted by footsteps and panting behind him. It was Jackie, smiling as always.

'All right, Dad?'

'Hello, hen.'

'You've got it looking lovely, Dad. I'll just put my wee plant down here.' Jackie's plant was small and pink, and fitted snugly in beside the vase.

'It was a right mess when I got here,' said Frank, 'Dead flowers all over the place.' Frank kicked a can that had blown into the grass at the side of June's grave.

'That's a shame.' They both drifted off into their own thoughts, then Jackie spoke quietly. 'Hiya, Mum. Hope you're okay. Are you having your favourite? Tea and an omelette? I bet you're having a cake as well! We're fine. My dad came round for dinner on Sunday. We had a roast chicken. It wasn't as good as yours, but he never left any on the plate.' Frank smiled as she continued. 'Tommy's fine, working away, you know, the bookies is very busy and that's good. Viv was there on Sunday as well, she's doing good. She's packed up eating the crisps and swapped it for Keep Fit, ha ha. She got a job with Avon. I got a new cot for the baby. My dad put it together on Sunday. What a laugh - oh! but what a mess! Cardboard everywhere! You'd have flipped your lid at the mess. Viv said her mum said that her next door neighbour has a wee go-chair that I can have for free, just needs a good clean. She's going to bring it round at the weekend. I still don't know what kind the baby is. It will be a nice surprise. I wish you were here, Mum, to see the baby coming. I wish you were here every day.' She paused in silence. 'Dad, do you want to say anything?'

Frank had stopped listening. He could see June to his left, standing down the hill, smiling, in her blue coat. Frank stared. He managed a weak smile. He willed her to walk up to the grave, to be closer to them, but she didn't. He knew if he moved towards her, she would disappear, so he had to keep her glance as long as he could.

'Dad...what are you looking at?' Jackie had her hand on his arm. 'Dad?'

'Yes, hen?'

'Was I going on a bit too much for you?'

'No, not at all. Your mum is listening. Keep talking, go on.' He motioned Jackie to face the gravestone again. He looked back to his left, and she was still there, down the hill. Jackie talked for another little while, then they both fell into a peaceful reflection. After about five minutes of Frank staring and Jackie quietly weeping, a loud shrill noise pierced the quietness. June disappeared.

It was Jackie, moaning, then taking shallow breaths, and then she drew in a quick, sharp breath. She stared hard at Frank. 'I think this is it, Dad.'

'Eh?'

'I've been getting some pains. Doctor says it might be Braxton Hicks, but it feels like more than that to me.'

'What's that? What should I do?'

'Is there a toilet here, Dad?'

'Well, did you not go before you came out?'

'Yes, but....Oh, Dad, that was sore. It's getting really sore now. The second bus was late, I shouldn't have walked. I think it could be starting.'

'Should we say a Hail Mary?'

'I need to sit down.'

'Where is there to sit? Oh, my God in heaven, help us!'

Jackie's breathing began to change to short little pants and long deep breaths.

'I think you need to get up, hen. We'll walk down to the main road, someone'll take us to hospital.' Frank started to look for another person in the graveyard, but there was nobody there. He didn't expect it to go this way. He thought Jackie would go into a nice hospital and have the baby, then he'd go in and visit, once everything was nice and tidy.

'Dad, phone an ambulance.'

'What?' Why did you have to come out here on your own? Where's Viv? What can I do? Can you hold it in for a minute? Somebody will come.'

'Go...down...to...that...phone box...' Jackie held her bump and panted. Her cheeks were as red as Cox's apples. Frank looked at the phone box at the bottom of the hill. He didn't want to leave Jackie but he knew he had to make the call.

'You definitely can't walk?'

'No! Get an ambulance, Dad! Move!'

Jackie's shouting kickstarted Frank's legs into motion. He ran in tiny steps down the hill to the phone. Every time Jackie wailed, Frank jolted but never turned around for fear of what he'd see.

Reaching the bottom of the hill, he opened the phone box door and was hit by the smell of stale urine.

'Oh, Christ save us! Mother of God!' He pulled a hankie from his pocket. Someone had stuck chewing gum to the number eight. Frank muttered to himself and picked up the receiver in the hankie, all the while avoiding the gum. He switched hands to use the hankie on his finger while he dialled 999. He then moved it to his nose to block the smell.

'Emergency services, which service do you require?' asked the telephone operator.

'Ambulance, please, to St Joseph's Cemetery, Airdrie. Quick as you can. There's a baby coming.'

'Is this a hoax?' said the telephone operator.

Frank realised that the hankie had made him sound like he had muffled his voice.

'No, sorry...' He removed the hankie. 'Look. I'm stuck in a graveyard with my daughter who is about to have a baby, there's not another soul around here.'

'Is it a ghostie baby?'

'Are you-'

'All right, calm down, just a wee joke. Ambulance is on its way.'

Frank walked back up the hill to see Jackie on all fours.

'I hope that Ambulance man has his foot to the floor. Maybe it's better if you sit up on something, you know, keep things in for a wee while.'

After a few frantic minutes of Frank uselessly consoling Jackie, he spotted an ambulance in the distance. As they were the only people in the graveyard, they were easy to see and the ambulance drove in through the gates straight up the hill to meet them. A paramedic unloaded a wheelchair.

'Right then. Jackie, will you be all right? I'll go home. Do you want me to phone Tommy?'

'You're leaving me? I need you!'

'What can I do, hen? I'm no good, I'm not used to...'

Jackie looked at Frank with frightened eyes as bright as the moon, and all at once, he saw her face at three years old.

'OK, I'll come for a wee while but I'll wait outside.' The paramedics loaded Jackie in the wheelchair into the back of the ambulance. 'Oh, June, where are you?' he stressed, looking around, then he climbed in behind Jackie.

The waiting room at the Maternity Ward was silent but for distant noises of phones ringing, doors swinging and trollies wheeling. Frank studied the line of blue chairs with torn holes exposing yellow foam. A curly-cornered *People's Friend* and *Reader's Digest* lay on the table. Frank stood up and paced. He wondered how long it was all going to take. He fingered a few of the foam holes, then chose the least torn chair, sat down, took a deep breath and threw his head back. He had gone down the hall to phone Tommy at the bookies but they said he had gone to lunch. He had visions of Tommy in the pub, with the good sandwiches Jackie had made him uneaten in a bin somewhere. He stood up and walked down the corridor to take the lift to the tea shop.

Frank was pleasantly surprised to see that the hospital prices were cheaper for the over sixty-fives. He fished out 20p for his drink and got himself a Wagon Wheel to go with it. As he sat at a table, two men, older than him, walked past, one on a Zimmer frame and the other attached to a drip that he wheeled along beside him. One smiled at him with brown teeth as they sat down at the next table. Immediately Frank could smell that hospital smell - like boiled potatoes that have been left in the pot and gone cold. It was getting up his nose. He loosened his tie and quickly finished off the last of the Wagon Wheel with a swig of lukewarm tea, then headed back up to the Maternity Ward, wondering what he might have caught.

The waiting room was still empty so he sat down in the same chair he was in before. His tongue poked at a bit of Wagon Wheel that had stuck in his tooth. He pulled the magazine table over with his foot and picked up the *People's Friend*. He stared at the picture of the thatched cottage on the front. *Wish I still had that Wagon Wheel wrapper, it would have done the job*. Frank considered tearing a corner off the *People's Friend* to pick his teeth, but as his hand approached the corner, he noticed the date on the front was a year ago. He thought of how many people had touched this *People's Friend* and threw it back down onto the table.

He settled down to think about what June would make of this waiting room. He was glad she spent her last days in a hospice and not in here.

He woke to a nurse gently shaking him. His neck was bent right back over the chair.

'Won't be long now. Jackie's well on her way - nine centimetres! She's doing fantastically well. One of the midwives will be back with some good news shortly!'

As the door slowly closed, Frank thought he heard screaming. He darted round in the chair, wondering if it was Jackie. He thought of her in there, alone.

# Frank

*What am I supposed to do? What do I know about babies? June, why are you not here? She's in the best hands. They know what they're doing.*

He took his hankie out to fold it and heard a new cry, louder this time. He bolted up out of the chair, through the flapping door.

'Which one is my daughter's room?' he asked a nurse.

'Changed your mind? She said you might. She's just in there.' The nurse motioned to the door beside the picture of a smiling Noddy carrying balloons.

Frank knocked on the door. Somebody was making a lot of noise in there.

No answer. He slowly pushed the door open a crack. He saw a bare leg on a bed and shut the door again.

More noise, people bustling about the room. He fished in his pocket for his hankie. He put it up to his eyes and pushed the door open wider.

'Can I come in? I'm not looking. Is she all right?'

Then he heard Jackie's voice.

'Dad? Oh, Dad! Come in!

A nurse placed a new-born baby into Jackie's arms. 'It's a girl,' the midwife announced, 'six pounds thirteen ounces and she's wide awake! My goodness, what a beauty.'

Jackie tried to sit up. Her hair was stuck to one side of her face and her gown wet with sweat. Her eyes sparkled.

Frank looked down at the most beautiful sight in the world. The baby was trying to focus. She had Jackie's eyes and tiny chin, the image of Jackie as a baby.

'A wee girl, Dad,' she said.

Frank squeezed at the hankie in his fist. The midwife took the baby to one side to check it over. Frank hugged Jackie.

'Are you all right, hen? I was worried about you.'

'So was I!' Jackie smiled a fresh smile, *the smile of a new beginning*, thought Frank, as all the heartache of the situation melted away.

'Did you hear from Tommy?' Jackie looked away from Frank, as if she knew the answer already.

'No.'

The midwife brought the baby back, wrapped tightly in what looked to Frank like a tea towel, but he realised was a hospital sheet. The baby was placed snugly into Jackie's arms.

'Her eyes are as big as old pennies!'

'Nose like a shirt button!' the two midwives commented as they moved around the bed, removing towels and replacing them.

'Are you feeling okay, Jackie? How about a nice

hot cup of sweet tea?' asked a midwife.

'Oh, now that sounds good!' smiled Frank.

'It was for Jackie, but we'll bring you one too, Granda!'

'Well, I liked the sound of the tea but now you've made me feel old!' Frank said. The women laughed and left the room to fetch the tea. Jackie and Frank looked down at the baby.

'She's an angel,' Frank croaked. He didn't know his voice was going to come out like that. 'What are you going to call her? Have you thought about a name?'

'I have.' She looked up to Frank, 'I thought... maybe we could call her after my mum? Baby June?'

'I think your mum would like that very much.' He squeezed Jackie's hand. The midwife came back in with tea and biscuits.

The sun shone brightly through the old nets on the window, and in the lemon coloured rays, Frank traced the silhouette of a beaming June, radiant in her light.

# MOVE IT

Tommy visited Jackie at the hospital once, after they kept her in for observation because she had needed two pints of blood. He brought her grapes, claiming she probably had enough cut flowers. He didn't allow her to bring any of her flowers to the flat when it was time to leave. 'They'll only die,' he said. She had to give them all to the midwives and nurses.

Frank saved the pink 'it's a girl' balloon he had bought for baby June. He carried it home proudly on the bus that day, his grin ever-present. Now a month later, it was floppy enough to stick a finger into and leave a dent, but the helium in it was still good to keep it high. It floated around his house of its own accord, a reminder of something good.

It didn't take long for Tommy to decide that Jackie and the baby had to leave. He struggled to cope almost as soon as they got home from the hospital. He couldn't stand the screaming at night and his flat had become a complete mess. Every surface in the kitchen was covered in bottles, nappies, towels and wet clothes. Nearly-dry baby clothes were draped on the radiators and there seemed to be an endless tower of dry, folded clothes on the bed, only tipped onto the floor for sleep, then put back in their piles on the bed during the day. Wet bibs and towelling nappies hung off every door handle. Different shapes of blanket and bedcover were thrown across the back of the couch. There was a buggy in the kitchen, more nappies on the spokes of his brand new clock, and he'd banged his toe on that cot - the one that Frank built - for the last time.

Tommy hated not being able to hear the television. He complained to Jackie that he could hardly hear *World In Action* over the sound of the washing machine on constant spin, and he resented her for remarking she'd never noticed him watching it before. The baby was never out of her arms.

After a month, he told Jackie that he thought it best she left for a while. Lack of sleep was affecting his work, he said, and he couldn't keep the money coming in if he wasn't able to work properly at the bookies. The flat was just too small for all this... 'stuff', he said. Jackie tried to protest that it was only early days, and showed him a bit in a book she got from the library that said that (whilst messy) this particular routine was good for the baby. He just wasn't interested. The more she protested, the less he wanted her there. Bachelor life, as he knew it, had ceased to exist, and he wanted his neat and tidy flat back. He dared not look at Jackie, a sight in a dressing gown. Since the baby was born, her hair had been falling out and her once-lush shiny brown bob clung to her face like limp noodles. Her sharp features now looked bony without make-up, and, strangely, whilst she had lost all the baby weight very quickly, she had gone, in his opinion, far too skinny. She had always been slender, but there were no curves any more and he could see her bones. In addition to this, she made no effort for him. The only time he ever saw her out of that dressing gown was when she changed into jogging bottoms to go to the shop for formula, and to top it all, he hadn't had a proper cooked meal in a good while. Everything they ate came out of the little freezer and was deep fried. As far as he was concerned, she chose the baby over their relationship, to be a mother first, moaner second, girlfriend last.

He told her that the move was only temporary, until she got back on her feet. They agreed that she and the baby should stay with her dad for a few months.

'Where there's more room for your...things,' he told her, as he moved some babygros off the sideboard to get to his aftershave.

# Frank

She smiled bleakly, a tired face, too young for the dark circles and pale skin. It was obvious that he just wanted her and the baby out, and she was too weak from sleepless nights to argue. Besides, she knew that when Tommy decided something, there was no going back.

When Jackie phoned to tell Frank that she was coming home, he acted like he felt sorry for her, but as he hung up, he did a little dance. He wanted Jackie home. He was lonely. He had made a mistake, pressuring Tommy to take her in for the sake of the baby, but what he had asked him to do was to look after her, and he wasn't doing that.

He was well aware that the local gossips would go to town on the news that she was coming home. 'She can't keep a man,' he imagined them saying, 'Tut, tut, no father for that wean.' Many thoughts raced through his head, what Mrs Morrisson might say - would she like it or not - she had been dropping a few bibs and babygros in for Jackie these past few weeks, showing a lot of kindness. This made Frank rub his head; was she really interfering or just being nice? He'd been eating an awful lot of her stews and pies.

Worst of all, what would the priest say about his single mother daughter?

'It's only temporary, Father!' he rehearsed his excuses to himself. 'Of course they'll be getting back together before long!' The priest had never stopped bothering Frank since they bumped into each other in the supermarket and Frank didn't like the 'Are you okay?' face he made when he saw him in the chippy queue, one of the more recent times that June had been there with him.

'Let them all talk,' he said to himself and scrolled his finger down the right hand side of the phone book alphabet. On arriving at 'V', he pushed the little metal button and it pinged open at exactly the right place. He dialled the number, carefully and slowly, reading the digits out loud to himself.

'Hello! Is that you, Viv? How's your dad? How's his leg? Aye, aye, that's good. Listen, you couldn't ask your dad if I could borrow his old van, could you? Aye? I'm to get Jackie and the baby...Naw... Not any more...Aye, that would be good, please. I know. He is, aye. Right, see you.' He hung up while Viv still talked.

Frank walked round to Viv's to get the van and picked her up along with it. They agreed he would take the belongings and she would take Jackie and baby June home in a taxi. She talked nonstop about what a 'rodent' Tommy was, and how he'd even

# Frank

tried it on with her, Jackie's best pal, and how she'd found the card but never said anything. Viv, and probably the whole town and every cousin, knew that the 'M' was 'Maureen'. Frank stayed silent, he didn't want to hear what was already hidden in his mind.

'Best not to mention any of that to Jackie,' he said, 'She's delicate enough.'

'Oh, no, she's far too fragile to hear that,' Viv agreed.

As they arrived at the flat, Frank was part-relieved, part-shocked that Tommy had everything ready - the cot was dismantled, the push-chair folded and the clothes and formula already in black bin bags. Jackie stood in the hall, rocking the baby.

'It's for the best,' he said to Frank.

Viv went with Jackie and baby June in a taxi, and Frank and Tommy loaded up the van.

'See you!' smiled Tommy, pushing the back doors shut and walking off back up to his flat. Then he turned and shouted 'Good bye, Frank!' sarcastically. Frank gave him a hard stare then climbed into the van.

'It's *Mister McNeill* to you,' Frank replied, before slamming the door, starting the engine and driving off as fast as he could.

Jackie, Viv and baby June were waiting at the front door when Frank drove up in the van. Baby June was screaming. Frank fumbled for his house keys.

'She's due a feed...' said Jackie, 'Look for her stuff in one of the black bags in the back, Dad.'

'Right, hen!' He opened the back of the van. Eight black bin bags were piled on top of the cot. He had no choice but to drag each one out and tear it open. After digging into the fourth bag, one by one the plastic bottles plopped out and rolled onto the ground. Impossible to catch, they trundled away down the street. Viv ran around collecting up two or three, grabbed Frank's keys and the big tub of formula and ran to the door. The two women and the baby darted into the house and through to the kitchen. Frank wiped the sweat off his brow and retrieved the last bottle and began unloading the other bags onto the pavement. He hadn't worked this hard since the railways, and it was a good feeling, to be needed. He hated having no purpose, even though he was dying on his feet with exhaustion. He hoped Jackie had the kettle on.

Jackie did indeed have the kettle on, and he heard the familiar click as he brought the bags into the hall. Putting the last one down, he walked into the kitchen hoping for tea, but instead saw a bottle full of hot milk bobbing in a jug of cold water. Baby

June continued to wail.

'Run the cold tap, Viv! Run it hard!'

'I'm running it!'

Jackie took the bottle out of the jug and held it under the cold water.

'Not long, my baby girl, not long, I know, yes, I do, and I know you're hungry.' Jackie stared into the baby's creased face, then re-adjusted her hold to move her onto her shoulder.

'Look at her holding her wee head up. She's so clever,' said Viv, encouragingly.

'She gets that from me!' said Frank, smiling. The baby wailed anew even louder, as if in protest at his bad joke. After what felt like an age of screaming, Jackie dotted milk out of the teat onto her wrist.

'That's it,' she said. She walked into the living room and sat on the couch. The only noise now was loud sucking.

'My God, she was starving!' said Viv.

'I know how she feels!' replied Frank. Viv filled the kettle and made three mugs of tea and found a packet of Garibaldis. They sat chatting about how lovely baby June was, and whether the cot should go upstairs or downstairs, and Tommy might change his mind and have her back soon, he'd be missing her.

Baby June fell asleep first, then Jackie's head

slowly flopped backwards, her mouth open, lightly snoring to the sound of Viv's comforting chatter, like the sound of a radio with the volume on low.

'Leave her, Frank,' said Viv. 'Let's get these cups in the sink and these bags unpacked.' Frank could think of nothing else but the pie and chips he was going to devour down at the Black Dog as soon as this was over.

It was one o'clock in the morning before he finished putting the cot together for the second time. Viv had gone home ages ago and Jackie and the baby were already tucked up in her single bed. Frank stood back to admire his handy work, still holding a screwdriver in one hand and the instructions in the other. The cot looked just like the picture on the paper; another triumph. He was getting good at this handyman game. He put his tools onto the mantelpiece and sat down. He picked up the picture of June.

'Look at that, eh? Not bad for an old fella!' The last word came out as a yawn and his head flopped backwards into the nest of the cushion, U-shaped from many years of naps.

He dreamt of June walking towards him with a tray of food in her hands. She was smiling and wearing her long nightie. He could see that the tray balanced a sausage sandwich on white bread with brown sauce and a perfect cup of hot tea. The smell was heavenly. She came and rested the tray on his knee, then sat on the arm of the chair with a hand on his shoulder.

`Eat this, Frank. You're doing great, son.`

Tommy was lying in bed beside Maureen, both of them smoking.

'When do you want me to start at the bookies? I can't wait to tell all the girls I'm jacking in that factory. My days of button checks are over! I'll be at work with my big stud!'

'It's just a part-time job; it's not confirmed yet, don't be telling anybody.'

'I won't! I'll wait until you say, Superman! You can do anything!' She squeezed his bicep.

'Aye, too true, darlin',' he replied, rubbing his arm, distractedly.

She had already hinted, or maybe boasted, to the girls at the factory that she might be making a 'career change' soon. Now that Jackie was out, step one was the bookies, step two a drawer at his flat.

'So she's gone, then?' Maureen asked, taking a deep drag.

'For now, aye,' he replied.

'Maybe I could come round to yours one day, then?' Maureen leaned over towards him on one elbow, her frilly viscose nightie dangerously near her lit cigarette, heavy with ash.

'Put that out before you set fire to the bed,' said Tommy.

'Oh - right.' She stubbed the cigarette out into a thick-bottomed glass ashtray already overflowing with cigarette butts. 'So, I was saying, I could come over to your flat -'

Tommy put both his hands up.

'She's only just out the door hours ago! For God's sake!'

Maureen looked back at him forlornly.

'Right then,' she huffed, folding her arms.

Tommy softened and leaned over. 'Give it time, Teacake, we'll be together, eventually.' He stroked her cheek. Maureen wondered if there were other women he did that to. She tried to ignore the jealous feelings rising in her throat.

Tommy sat up and put his shirt on.

'Already? It's only six o'clock. The birds aren't singing yet!' She patted the space beside her, hopefully.

'Got to get home. Can't be seen in the same clothes, can I? People will talk.'

'So? You're a free man now.'

'Not yet I'm not. She won't let me off that easily. Mark my words. She'll be round, looking for money.' He stood up and tightened his belt around his trousers as he continued his rant. 'Did you know its hair has come in red? Since when was there red hair in my family? Or in hers, for that matter?' He slid his watch onto his wrist. 'Might not even be mine! For all I know, it could be Ginger Terry's!'

'Never mind that. Let me come round to your flat tonight. I can cook you a nice dinner -'

'Oh, for God's sake, Maureen, give it a rest. I didn't think you were the clingy type,' he snapped.

'Clingy? How is frying a bit of steak and making a few tatties clingy?'

'Frying a steak, staying the night, losing an earring in the bed, got to come back round for it, leaving tights in the drawer...and then suddenly it's booties and bibs? No thanks, I just had that. I don't need it again, no way.'

Maureen sat bolt upright.

'That was cruel, Tommy. I can't have children! You know that! On account of my -'

'Age.'

'That's not true! And anyway, I don't see why we have to hide things! Most people round here know about us!'

'Who? Who knows about us?' He leaned in across

the bed. 'I'll tell you who knows about us,' he whispered, 'Nobody. Nobody knows about us, Maureen, got that? Nobody.' A tiny bit of spittle landed on her cheek. He paused, then thumbed it away, a little too hard. 'Let's leave that thought of your job at the bookies for now, shall we?' He slid his jacket on over his shirt, pocketed his keys and walked out. The door banged.

Maureen opened her bedside cabinet drawer. She tossed out a few empty fag packets and retrieved a six pack of Tunnock's tea cakes. She tore the cardboard box open and removed a teacake. She unwrapped the foil, throwing it on the floor before opening her mouth wide and forcing the entire teacake inside. Crumbs bounced down from her mouth to the frills of her nightie as she opened a second teacake.

# GUARDIAN ANGELS

Frank felt like his prayers had been answered having the two girls back at home. Nobody mentioned Tommy, and this suited Frank perfectly. Months passed quickly with a baby, and Tommy's name got lost.

Jackie was back at work in the hospital, so Frank's new job as Granda Frank was to look after the baby during the day, and Jackie to take over at night. Jackie fed the baby in the evening at eleven o'clock, then again at four o'clock, before she got up at seven to go to work at the hospital. Being twenty-one meant that she noticed the effect of disturbed sleep less than he did. In fact, she appeared to look younger and fresher every day in Frank's opinion, bouncing out of bed, white shoes laced, biting on toast while feeding baby June, all with a smile. The dark circles under her eyes had faded and she had gained a little bit of weight, now that she was back to eating cakes and biscuits with the other nurses in their breaks. She was now much less bony than when she arrived, but still trim. Her baby bump was completely gone.

Frank held the baby and admired his daughter's

tall slender frame standing gracefully at the bay window while she watched for the bus, like a gazelle looking into the woods.

'Right, that's me, I can see the bus coming. See you tonight, Dad. Bye-bye, sweetheart, bye-bye! Wave bye-bye to Mummy.'

Frank made baby June's hand wave to the back of Jackie and they watched her together as she ran out the door to the bus stop. The house was quiet.

'Time to get on with our day, eh? Come on, now, you and Granda will see what we can get up to.'

Frank enjoyed his time with baby June during the day. Occasionally Mrs Morrisson dropped off a sponge cake or some warm scones, and she'd stay a while and wash the teacups after they ate. He started to look forward to her little visits as sometimes she'd insist he'd head upstairs for forty winks in the afternoon while she watched the baby.

He had learned new skills, his biggest challenge learning to cook a dinner. He was forever burning the Findus Crispy Pancakes and dropping potato peelings onto the floor, which later he'd have to sweep up, as he learnt how to clean and sweep, too. He'd never cooked when June was alive, and there was certainly none of this frozen stuff he now had to fry. Everybody was exhausted, but happy. Frank spent a little less time thinking of June, to the point where he felt a stab of guilt when he noticed her picture on the mantelpiece.

'I'm just busy, you know, that's all,' he'd say.

It's okay, you carry on, he'd hear. She hadn't visited him for a while, but he still dreamt of her vividly, until the dreams were punctuated by the dawn wails of baby June, demanding the attention of the street.

Now seven months old, baby June (never 'June') was only waking once in the night, as she worked through the pain of four new teeth, two top and two bottom. Frank thought she looked like a cartoon baby with her four half teeth and one tufted curl of bright red hair.

When Jackie was at home, she spent a lot of time with the baby in her arms or cuddled into her shoulder. Baby June smiled more than most and had the brightest green eyes that beamed like emeralds directly from her face to Frank's heart. One smile from her was all it took to forget the tiredness and the chores he faced for the day.

His habits were changing and he stopped wearing a tie (he'd worn a tie every day since retirement, June always liked him to be smart, never scruffy). The labels on the back were permanently wet with frayed edges damaged by baby-drool.

Now eating solids, baby June devoured creamed

porridge from the jar. Frank struggled with getting the food into her mouth. When Jackie fed her, she ate it no problem. When Frank tried to feed her, she'd put her fingers into the bowl to explore the porridge, then flick and smear it all over the high chair. The only thing that helped was to give her a few wooden clothes pegs and make a train on the tray. Then he could scoop up big spoonfuls and choo-choo them into her mouth, scraping the plastic spoon against her new bottom teeth. The pegs didn't always work, and often he'd have porridge or mashed potatoes or custard encrusted into what was left of his hair, and a litter of pegs on the carpet. He didn't care. He loved the feel of her soft little fingers exploring the bald part of his head. He'd take her hand and squeeze the plumpness gently, pausing to look at the seams on her wrists and marvel at her dainty fingers, like little chips. It was one of their routines for him to tickle her while she sat in the high chair, the sound of her throaty forty fags-a-day-laugh filling an empty house with bright baby joy and happiness.

He liked to take her out everywhere, his badge of pride. Who cared what they said about Jackie not being with Tommy? He had no time to think about that any more.

It took him two hours to get her fed, washed, and

changed into whatever outfit Jackie had left out for her. His stiff clumsy fingers struggled with the small poppers on the legs of the babygros, and he'd often put her into the pram with one stud clicked to the stud below and triangle-shaped gaps all the way down.

This particular Thursday was sunny, so Frank decided that the two of them were going to take a trip out, and he got himself ready upstairs in the bathroom. He shaved as the baby sat on the floor, watching him intently. He found her a pleasant distraction even though everything took three times as long, as he made noises and funny faces as the Bic razor slid down his face and she bounced with glee on the rug.

'This is Granda's comb, now don't you chew it!' he offered, and she grabbed the blue plastic comb and took it straight to her mouth, laughing.

'I said, don't you chew that!' he teased, 'that's Granda's good comb!'

'Da-da-da-da!' she replied, drooling onto her new 'Trouble' bib.

'You're a wee rascal!' He smiled into the mirror and rinsed off his face. There were fresh cracks around his eyes. The mirror was always a disappointment and never displayed the younger man he felt inside. Staring back at him was a tired old face, a paler, more wrinkled version of his once-handsome self. Less hair, in fact not much left at all now, all grey. He rubbed his belly, tight against his vest. He looked away, back to baby June. *Please God, just let everything be all right inside me,* he thought, and his mind flashed back to June, talking to him from her hospice bed.

'Look after yourself when I'm gone. Eat good dinners.'

'You're going nowhere. They'll find a donor soon.'

He plunged his face down into the sink and threw water on it from the tap, trying to block out the voice of the doctor when June was first diagnosed.

'I'm sorry, Mr McNeill. At her age...she's further down the list...' He felt choked. The familiar tsunami-surge of hurt rushed from his heart to his eyes. For a second he felt her; she was behind him, holding him close, her arms around his shoulders, leaning her head into his back. He could smell her sweet scent...but then...she was squeezing him, tapping his shoulder, hard. He opened his eyes and looked up to see baby June with the comb half way down her throat. In one swift motion, he removed the comb from her mouth and smacked her back. She looked confused, crumpled her face and held it there, temporarily in silence, then let out a long wail, followed by loud, machine gun cries. Tear-shaped drool balanced on her bottom lip. He checked inside her mouth and her throat, which was easy to do as it was as wide as the Clyde, and this gave him an ample view of her beautiful, undamaged tonsils.

'You're all right. Oh, thank God.' He scooped her up into his arms and turned and looked at the sink a little hopefully, but his wife wasn't there. Adrenaline pumped deep down into his legs, making every muscle tight. The baby cried into his chest and he held her close and kissed her curl.

'Granda's got you. It's all right now. It's all right.' A tear fell down his cheek and he dried his whole face with the hand towel in one hand. 'Come on, we'll go get Granda dressed. No more Granda's comb!' He picked up the comb and threw it into the sink. 'All gone,' he told her, dotting her tiny nose with his finger. 'Let's go out now.'

He took her into the bedroom and handed her a soft teddy. Immediately, she took the teddy's ear to her lips.

'Everything goes in the mouth, eh?' he said, shaking his head. 'We'll go to your favourite place. We'll go and get a pie at The Black Dog. That's right! The Black Woof-Woof!' He could see her eyes begin to smile, encouraging his words. 'You want a pie? Oh no, you can't have a pie! No, no! No pie for you now. Babies don't get pies. Banana for you. Banana pie! Are you having a banana pie?'

A smile shaped like an orange slice spread across her wet face. Pleased with himself, he tried on a navy jacket, paused to finger the lapels and thought briefly of squashed banana, then changed it to a waterproof mac. Downstairs, he lay baby June carefully into her pram.

'That's it now,' he said.

She lay on her back staring at the line of ducks on the white string of elastic across the hood. Frank tucked a pink shawl over her legs and fastened her little pale pink double-breasted coat tightly. He tied a knitted pom-pom hat under her chin. It didn't really matter if the babygro didn't fasten underneath. Nobody would see. He packed the pram bag with a bottle of formula, a banana and a nappy. He quickly checked inside her mouth and throat again before they left. As he put a dummy in her mouth to suck, the grandfather clock in the hall chimed twice.

'It says here that Elizabeth Taylor had eight husbands!' Jackie paused.

'I'd say she had the right idea. Read it out loud, please, Jackie.'

It was unusually quiet in the ward, so Jackie was

sitting reading a magazine at the bedside of her favourite patient, seventy-seven year old Bridget. Bridget had been brought in to the Geriatric Ward with severe bladder complications and a stubborn infection that had spread to her kidneys. She had been in Jackie's ward for a month. Jackie didn't know too much more about her medical problems; as an auxiliary nurse, she didn't need to. She was frequently reminded of her job: to keep the patients clean and comfortable and assist the nurses with any other duties they required.

'*Screen siren Elizabeth Rosemond Taylor was married eight times. Her first husband was notorious socialite and heir to the Hilton fortune, Conrad Hilton Junior. Fond of gambli-*'

'He had an affair, you know,' Bridget interrupted.

'Did he?'

'With his mother.'

'What?' Jackie let the magazine drop to her knees. 'With his mother?'

'You know her!'

'I know her?'

'Course you do. She had a rake of shoes...no, not her, that's the other one...she had...cats, that's it.'

'His mum had cats?'

'No, she wasn't his mother. She was just the father's wife. Oh, now, what's her name now...'

'Which one?'

'The father's wife!' Jackie could hear the insistent tone of Bridget's voice but was still none the wiser. Bridget's logic never followed a straight path, but weaving the way was part of their ritual.

'Maybe it will say in the magazine, hold on.' Jackie lifted it back to her eyes and continued: '*Fond of gambling, drinking and excessive partying, Hilton Jnr's marriage to* National Velvet *star Taylor came to an end after only nine months in 1951, when his behaviour turned abusive. Hilton Jnr was reported to have had an affair with his step-mother, Zsa Zsa Gabor, in 1944.*'

'There you go! Zsa Zsa Gabor! I knew it!' A triumphant smile spread across Bridget's face. 'Zsa Zsa Gabor!' she repeated, tapping her arm on the bed, an ever-present clean tissue tucked tight inside her fist.

'You know everything, Bridget!' Jackie grinned widely. She stood up and put the magazine on the chair and went around the bed, tucking in sheets.

'Not too tightly now, Jackie,' she said.

'I know, Bridget, I won't tuck it too tightly,' she reassured her. The Staff Nurse walked past Bridget's bed, checking the watch on her top pocket.

'She's a guardian angel, this one,' Bridget said

loudly to the Staff Nurse as she passed.

'Oh, I know!' said the Staff Nurse, continuing on her way. Jackie tidied around Bridget's bed and re-filled her water jug.

'Tell me now, how's baby June?' Bridget asked.

'She's great, she's got four teeth.'

'Ah, I'd love to see her.'

'I'll try to bring her in, one day.'

'You will not bring her into this old place! Sure she could catch anything!'

Jackie drained Bridget's catheter and took the bucket away to flush and clean. She returned five minutes later with a cup of hot tea.

'Just a spot of milk, how you like it, same as myself.'

'Ah, bless you now,' she sipped, 'Nice and hot. I don't like a lot of milk in my tea.'

'Me neither.'

Jackie knew exactly how Bridget liked her tea because Bridget told her every day.

'Sure, any man would be lucky to have a beautiful young girl like you,' she sipped, holding the cup. 'They'll be snapping you up now you've got your figure back! You look like a teenager! A model!'

'I do not!' Jackie laughed.

The hospital porter passed through the ward with his mop and bucket. About the same age as Jackie, he had blonde floppy curly hair cut into the shape of a mushroom, and he blushed a lot around nurses. Bridget eyed him, then Jackie.

'Hello, Daniel!' said Bridget, loudly. 'Mopping away, there?'

Daniel smiled, mumbled 'Aye', then looked to the floor.

'Bless him, he's a good young lad,' said Bridget. 'He's single, too, you know!' Jackie shook her head and folded a sheet. 'Tell me now, is there any man yet?' Bridget enquired in her familiar stage whisper.

'No, no man, the baby keeps me too busy.'

'Not that Jack-the-Lad. Now, don't let that Jack-the-lad come calling again.'

'I won't.' Jackie shook her head.

'Make sure you don't, now.' Bridget sipped her tea. 'Beautiful,' she muttered. 'You makes a lovely cup of tea! It always tastes better when another person makes it. She makes a lovely cup of tea, you know, Daniel.' She handed the cup and saucer to Jackie, passed a tiny burp, chuckled to herself, then closed her eyes. Daniel smiled at Jackie over his mop, blushing under his curls.

'Carry on, Jackie, please,' said the Staff Nurse, 'Mrs Williamson needs her bath.' She walked briskly out of the ward.

'Yes, Staff Nurse Mary,' replied Jackie to the back

of her head. Jackie looked at Daniel, as he mopped.

'A million dollars you look.' Bridget said, with her eyes closed.

Jackie smiled and tidied up the magazines on Bridget's table, then left the ward to prepare Mrs Williamson's bed bath.

Bridget opened one eye, looked around, and then closed it again.

# GRANDA'S PRIDE

Baby June's eyelids grew heavy as the pram trundled down the street. With a tight grip on the bar, Frank looked for some bumpy ground to roll the wheels over, just to watch her fat cheeks wobble over some wonky paving or a manhole cover. Her dummy was plunged deep into her mouth as tight as a plug in a full bath. Frank felt proudly in control, looking for people to look at him.

As the baby's head lolled to one side, the pompom hat remained facing front so her face was buried into the side of the wool. He stopped walking, put the pram brake on, and untied the hat from under her chin. He lifted the side flap away from her face so that she could breathe freely. He left the hat on top of her head, untied. He was still getting to grips with this carriage. The baby's tiny size meant that when he went down a kerb, her body slid to the top, and when he went up a kerb, she slid all the way down to the bottom, her face disappearing from view. Frank had to keep stopping to readjust her position so that he could see her face, but he was conscious that too much fussing would wake her up. He decided to just leave her to slide up and down, fast asleep. Luckily, the hat seemed to remain stationary at the top, the wool stuck to the cotton sheet like Velcro. The pompom had been knitted by Mrs Morrisson and was the size of a watermelon, but it made a good soft buffer for her soft crown against the hard plastic.

Reaching the Black Dog, he hesitated, wondering if he should leave the pram outside, but then he saw the barmaid, who ushered him in, rushing from behind the bar to hold the door open.

'Come in, come in, come in,' she fussed, 'Aww! Would you look at that! She's gorgeous. Aww, look at her! Baby June! Och, June, och that's nice...all peaceful...Oh, now isn't that just the nicest...TURN THAT DOWN! TURN IT DOWN! NOW! JOHN! PUT IT OFF! NOW! YOU'LL WAKE THE WEAN!' she roared. Somebody had put the jukebox on and the barmaid's voice changed from a gentle sweetness into a caveman grunt. A small man leapt off his stool and dashed behind the optics to seek out the jukebox volume and silence The Dave Clark Five. Baby June remained asleep through the whole ordeal and the barmaid took the pram off Frank, wheeled it over to a table by the bar flap and clicked on the brake, like an expert mother. She turned back to Frank.

'Honest to God!' she moaned, 'some folk have got no idea! Och, look at her though, sound asleep. Eyelashes like paintbrushes! All the laddies will be chasing you round, eh? Better watch out, this one will be a wee heartbreaker, so she will! Now, a pint, is it? And I'll say you'll be hungry, eh?' Frank nodded like a shy toddler. 'We've a lovely steak pie today. Let me go heat that up for you right now.' She tied an apron around her waist and strode behind the bar, continuing to talk to herself whilst pulling a pint and warming a dish. She was happy to have some work to do. Frank checked on baby June, still fast asleep, dummy out. The bar was nice and quiet, soothing her dreams.

'That's lovely, thank you,' said Frank as the barmaid put the plate onto the bar. Frank took a sip of the pint and cut into the pie. Steam rose from under the buttery pastry and the smell of gravy-covered Scottish beef filled his nose. He scooped a bit of the filling and pastry onto the back of the fork and into his mouth. The chunk of steak was far too hot and he burnt his tongue. He stole an urgent sip of the sweet pint to soothe his taste buds. The barmaid disappeared into the back and the other men looked into their pints. June appeared in the seat beside him.

'You're back!' he whispered, fork to mouth.

She wagged her finger. He knew she was telling him to *slow down, blow on it*, but he was too hungry to care. He cut the pie up in squares and lifted the lid of the pastry off and put it on the side of the plate so that the steak would cool quicker. Then he looked at June and raised his eyebrows. She nodded.

'Any brown sauce, hen?' he shouted through to the back in a loud stage whisper. The barmaid nodded and the *Daddies* sauce slid down the bar. Frank squeezed the sauce all over the pie in a zigzag and proceeded to eat the entire pie so quickly that, by the time he was finished, the plate was still warm. June shook her head and smiled.

'Not as good as yours!' he smiled back.

After two slices of bread and butter and a further pint, one of the ducks on the elastic started to wobble. Baby June never woke up crying, she just wriggled around under the tight pink blanket like a baby bird pecking its way out of a shell. One, then two legs would escape, followed by one arm, then the other, and a mild grizzle, to let Frank know it was time to pick her up, which he would, just after he peeked under the hood.

'Who's in there? Who's that? Is that you awake? Is it?' he smiled, his big face filling the square-shaped hood. Her smile beamed back at him, eyes fresh and wide from perfect sleep. Her legs began to bump against the mattress excitedly, and the blanket lay crumpled in a pile on her belly. Frank put it to one side and slid his arms under hers to pick her up. Her hair was static and stood up and out like a dandelion clock. He tried to pat it down but it bounced back up again.

'Are you hungry?' he asked, unbuttoning her coat. 'Are you hungry? Are you hungry?' He kissed her face and breathed in her baby smell, a mix of formula and flower petals; she always carried a hint of Jackie's perfume.

'Is that her awake? Och, look, she's awake, och, look at that, look at her, give us a wee cuddle...' the barmaid started, moving in.

'I'll just give her the bottle first.'

'I'll do it, if you like!' The barmaid leaped forward eagerly, her wearied face in desperate need of an escape from beer and the mundane.

'You can hold her for one wee second.' He reluctantly passed the baby over to the barmaid whilst he searched for the bottle and the banana. He shook the bottle up and motioned to the barmaid to hand her back quickly as she was getting fidgety. Getting her into position, he put the bottle in her mouth.

'Oh heck, I've forgot a bib!'

# Frank

'No bother – I've just the thing. JOHN, GO GET US A BAR TOWEL FROM BEHIND THE BAR.'

Again, the small man leaped up out of his stool behind the bar and brought back a damp towel.

'NOT THAT ONE, YOU CLOWN! A CLEAN ONE! Och, I'll get it myself...' She walked off behind the bar and retrieved a clean towel. 'Fresh out the machine,' she said, tucking it under baby June's chin. Frank thought it had a whiff of stale cigarettes but he wasn't about to complain.

Baby June chugged on her bottle contentedly. She was always starving after a good sleep. After three ounces, he had to yank the bottle out of her mouth. Reluctant to give it up, she let out a wail, but Jackie had warned him to burp her every three ounces, and June was watching. As soon as she was upright, she let out a massive belch.

'Oh ho!' said Frank, 'have you been on the Guinness?' He put the bottle back in her mouth. 'She's some wean, eh?' he said to June, in passing. Frank felt a little glow; a happy warmth that he hadn't felt in years. He looked to June and, maybe it was the beer, but his heart felt fuller than a Christmas Day stomach. June smiled.

The pub door blasted open. June disappeared. It was Tommy, staggering. He weaved his way to the bar.

'Merry Christmas, beautiful!' he slurred to the barmaid.

'It's April, and I think you've had enough. Go on home now, son.' Tommy caught sight of Frank, then the baby. It looked like he was going to say something, then changed his mind.

'This pub is SHITE ANYWAY,' he shouted directly at Frank, then left by the side door.

'No mind him. Bloody eejit,' said the barmaid, drying glasses.

Frank burped baby June one more time and packed her back into the pram with her dummy. Time to go - Jackie would be home from work soon.

Jackie walked through the door and the phone was ringing.

'Hi, Viv! A party? Oh, my God, this is so exciting, Viv! When did you decide that? Did he? Oh, this will be magic! What are you wearing? What will I bring? What do you want for a present? NO, VIV, I'M NOT GETTING YOU THAT. NAW! HA HA HA! Is he? Aye, I might! No not really. Well, there is somebody, aye, och, just a guy from work. I might bring him. Oh, this is great. I haven't had a night out in ages. Right, then. Who, my dad? No way, I'll need him to babysit! If he comes, I'll have no sitter! Aye, I suppose she would...I'll ask Mrs Morrisson. I think she'd jump at the chance. Och, well, we'll wait and see. I can't wait! Okay, see you soon!' Jackie heard the noise of the key in the door. 'I'd better go. Ring you soon! Bye!' She hung up and turned towards the grandfather clock.

The door swung open and Frank pushed the pram in over the step, closing the door behind him.

'I didn't expect to see you home at this time, hen!'

'Sister let me off a wee bit early today! Hiya, baby! Aww, look who's awake with a big smile for her mummy! Aww, look at you. I missed you too, my wee baby. Och, you're just lovely...What's that sm- Can I smell fags off her?'

'Well, I just treated myself to my lunch in the Black Dog. Somebody was smoking but they were a few tables away, near the snug bar.'

'Fair enough. What did you have?'

'Steak pie.'

'Was it nice?'

'Aye, no bad.' Frank felt sheepish, like he'd been caught stealing a pencil from John Menzies. He had tried to get home before Jackie. He didn't know why he felt guilty about getting caught and he wasn't sure if he should tell her he'd seen Tommy.

'It's all right, Dad. You're entitled to go out and have your lunch, for goodness sake. Did she take much of her bottle?'

'The whole lot! And a banana!'

'Good girl! I'll give this one a quick bath, then get her bottle.' She turned to go up the stairs and paused. 'Guess what? Viv's having a birthday party! Last minute thing! This Saturday!'

'Is she? Where...?'

'Up at the Workmen's. It will be a right laugh! I'm getting her something nice. You're invited!'

'Me? Am I? Oh, that'll be good!'

'Aye! We'd better get a babysitter,' Jackie sang, climbing a few more stairs. 'Oh, and Dad - I might bring somebody from work, okay?'

'Who?'

'Just somebody. Nobody you know. A guy.'

'Oh right, aye, fine.'

Frank went to hang his coat on the hook and the front doorbell rang. He never normally heard the doorbell. Nobody really came to the front door. Any visitors came to the back door, gave a knock, opened the door and came in. That's the way June had liked it. An open door. He looked through the spyhole. It was the priest. He patted down his jumper and opened the door.

'Hello, Father!'

'Hello, Frank, how are you?'

'Very well, would you like to come in? Jackie is just bathing the baby.'

# Frank

'Ah, good, I was hoping to catch her as well. Okay, so I'll come in for a minute and wait.'

Frank stepped back to let the large priest enter. Although he wore the dog collar, it was odd to see him out of his vestments in a regular brown raincoat, looking like any ordinary person. As he removed his coat to hang it, Frank noticed the priest's feet and recoiled. He was wearing sandals. His thick brown toenails reached out from under the straps. Frank wondered with some disgust when they had last been cut. Could the priest even reach the toenails any more with his weight? Or did somebody come to clip them for him? How had he let his toenails get to that state? Who has toenails like that? Surely he could see them in the bath. Maybe he can't wear shoes any more on account of the toenails. Maybe they slice through the leather.

'Frank?' said the priest.

'Aye,' Frank replied, absentmindedly.

'What are you looking at?'

'Eh? Sorry, Father, what did you say?'

'I asked what you were looking at?'

'Just the carpet.'

'The carpet?'

'Wee bit of baby sick there, I think.' Frank licked his thumb and rubbed the carpet. Closer, the toenails were the colour of nicotine. He didn't want to look but he couldn't help it.

'That's got it, I think!' said Frank, rubbing at nothing.

'Oh! Hello, Father! I never knew you were coming?' Jackie was walking down the stairs, baby June in her arms with a hooded towel on her head, in a fresh nappy and buttoned onesie with giraffes all over it.

'I hope it's not too inconvenient? Frank was supposed to ring the parish house - remember, Frank?'

'Oh! It slipped my mind, Father.'

'It's not inconvenient at all!' Jackie passed by, kicking her dad's shoes under the phone table.

'Come in, come through...' she beckoned. The priest walked around Frank and through to the living room. Frank was still bent down.

'Dad! Get up!' Jackie motioned from the doorway.

Frank stood up and walked into the living room. The priest took a seat across two cushions of the couch. Both cushions bent upwards at the edges, like the wings of a jumbo jet. Jackie appeared with tea in a cup and saucer and a few custard creams on a side plate.

'What can we do for you, Father?' she asked. Frank wondered where his tea was, but didn't ask.

# Frank

The custard cream made a loud snap as the priest took a bite. His repetitive crunching was as loud as road works.

'I'm here about the christening. Do you have something in mind?'

'Christening? What christening? Jackie, did you make me a cup?' said Frank, with a bewildered look.

'I'll just boil the kettle again,' she said with a fake smile, leaving the room.

# GOING UP

'We were just talking about that, weren't we, Dad?' Jackie returned to the room. The priest watched as she rubbed baby June's hair dry, then brushed it with a silver brush with soft bristles.

'That's right! Of course we were! We need to get the wean baptised! Just finding the time, you know, Father. Jackie, would you mind passing me one of those custard creams, please, dear?' Frank motioned to the plate. Jackie put the brush down, stood up with the baby on her hip, picked up the plate and took it over to her dad. 'One!' she mouthed. Frank knew what she was whispering but slid two off the plate.

'Tea?' he mouthed back at her.

'I think I left your tea in the kitchen!' Jackie put the plate of biscuits back down in front of the priest, lay the baby on the floor with a soft rattle and walked back into the kitchen. Baby June's face crumpled at the sight of her mother leaving the room again.

'Now, now,' Frank fussed, 'here you go.' He handed the baby one of her favourite toys, June's old empty spectacle case. She took it and rolled it over and over in her hands, exploring the trail of the paisley pattern. 'She loves that! Wait to see - straight in the mouth...there you go!'

Frank chuckled and bit into his biscuit. It felt dry on his tongue without the tea. He put the remains of the biscuit next to the other one on the wooden arm of his chair, stained with an Olympic design of tea rings, and waited for Jackie to return. He could see Father Cleary's toenails out of the corner of his eye, so focused his attention onto the baby.

'You like that, don't you, eh? Eh? Give Granda a wee bit!' he teased, laughing. The baby started to laugh. Father Cleary slurped his tea loudly. Jackie came back in with a cup of tea and a fresh bottle for the baby. She sat down on the edge of the couch.

'Don't get her worked up, Dad! I've told him about that at this time of night, Father.' Jackie's smile was present on her lips but not in her eyes. She picked up the baby, removed the spectacles case from her mouth and replaced it with the bottle. Baby June relaxed into the comfortable corners of her mother and welcomed a familiar milky doze. Frank dunked his custard cream in the tea and it melted on his tongue.

'Mmm. The biscuit's nicer when you dunk it, Father.'

'What dates did you have in mind, Jackie?' the

priest boomed. 'I happen to have the church diary with me...'

'Oh, right, em...' Jackie fumbled with the bib while the priest announced loudly:

'The available dates are: 17th of this month, or I've got the 30th....there's a wedding cancellation... that was supposed to be a big do...cold feet apparently...although he says her feet were warm enough with the manager from that electrical shop.'

'That place with the TVs in the window? Stepek?'

'I believe so, Frank, yes.' The priest leaned in, 'He says it started with a free Betamax... and then went on from there.' The priest tutted. Frank tutted. Jackie joined in the tutting. Frank tutted louder again and shook his head.

'I wonder if it was a remote control Betamax he gave her?' Frank picked up the plate of biscuits.

It was rare for the priest to gossip like this so Frank offered him another custard cream, hoping he'd go on to reveal whose wedding it was. Father Cleary held his hand up and waved the plate away. Frank reversed backwards until he reached his chair and sat down, plate on lap. Somehow, there was only one custard cream left.

'I've also got the 14th of next month, or the 21st...'

'21st sounds good. Dad, do you think that's enough time?'

'I don't know, hen. You know better than me about these things...' Frank dunked his second biscuit.

'Well, you'll have to know about these things now, Frank!' the priest said, pointing around the room, 'Jackie can't do it all by herself! One of these modern men you'll have to be, fetching and cooking and carrying and all that...'

'Oh, don't you worry, Father. He does his fair share,' nodded Jackie, 'I've got him well trained.'

The priest finished writing in the diary and slammed it shut. He stood up.

'21st it is, then! Service after twelve o'clock Mass. I'll see you ALL back at church this weekend. I've a home visit to do a few streets away so I'll thank you for your hospitality and be off. Plans afoot! Moving on! Keeping busy. That's the ticket!' Jackie walked into the hall to get the priest's coat whilst still feeding the baby.

June appeared where the priest had been sitting. Frank was startled. She looked fainter than before. The priest noticed Frank's face. He turned around and looked at the couch.

'Maybe put the fire on now. Getting chilly. No need to see me out. Good night, all!' The door slammed shut behind him and Frank stared at June. He'd never noticed any chill.

Outside, the priest stood, looking in the window. He thought he saw a another figure on the couch. He'd seen this type of thing before. It was faint, but it was there all right, although his mother always insisted he had a strong imagination. He shook his head and reached into his pocket, pulling out a custard cream. With a loud snap, he crunched, chewed for a few seconds, and then popped the second half of the biscuit in his mouth before the first half had been swallowed. He walked out and fastened the hatch on the gate.

'I'm off to put her down,' Jackie whispered through the door. Baby June was asleep in Jackie's arms, one arm flopped straight south. She carried the baby up the stairs. Frank stood up and closed the door quietly.

'Hello love,' he said. June pointed upwards.

'Up? Is it time for me to go with you? Is this...my time?' he asked her, with a hard swallow of sweet tea crumbs.

'Am I to go with you? Up, "there", with "him"? I know...I mean...I know I've not been at Mass in a wee while, but we're going this Sunday. Jackie just booked the christening, for God's sake. I mean, for goodness sake. I didn't mean that, I meant for goodness sake. Tell him. Sure you must have heard...'

June pointed up. A tear rolled down Frank's cheek.

'Right now?' he asked, 'Surely not..?'

June shook her head and smiled. She pointed up again.

'Not to heaven? Am I dying? I feel all right. I mean, there was that sore toe but...'

June shook her head.

'I'm not dying?'

June shook her head.

'Am I sick?'

June shook her head.

'Is Jackie sick...the wean? Oh, no, please don't tell me...'

June shook her head and pointed up.

'Well, what are you pointing up for?'

June pointed up again.

'Up the stair?'

She nodded and pointed up again, this time a little higher.

'Well, if it's not the big house, and it's not up the stair...what's between up the stair and the big house?'

She pointed up again.

'The loft?'

She nodded.

'You want me to go in the loft?'

June nodded.

'Och, no, not the loft...it's all dusty and...wait... what for?'

June pointed upwards and began to fade.

'Wait!'

She smiled and pointed up, nodding.

'Wait a minute!'

June held her finger to her lips. Frank dropped his voice to a whisper.

'What do you want me to go in the loft for?'

`Look, Frank. You'll find it,` he heard. June pointed up and faded away.

'June...wait...I don't know...'

The door opened.

'Are you all right, Dad?'

'What? I'm fine, aye.' Jackie stood, slightly frozen, arms by her sides.

'What was the noise?'

'What noise?'

'I heard you talking.'

'That wasn't me. I put the radiogram on for a minute. It was that guy...him that sounds like me. I turned it off. C'mon, we'll get this placed tidied up.'

'Oh, okay. I'll do that. You sit down. Put the telly on.' She led him over to his chair and sat him down, plumping the pillow behind him. 'I worry about you sometimes.'

'I'm all right!'

Jackie busied herself straightening up the cushions on the couch. She put the TV on. It was Judith Chalmers on a beach.

'What about Father Cleary, eh? Turning up like that? It's a good job I had Hoovered. Still, that's us got a christening to plan. We'll need godparents! One will do, Viv can be the godmother. Do you think? Not Tommy. I'm not inviting Tommy. He's not even a Catholic! He can forget it. What will we do for food? Sausage rolls and that? Aye. Do it here. Oh, it's so exciting! We've got Viv's party and we've got the christening! Eh, Dad? I'll need to get something to wear! I'll go to Airdrie market tomorrow before I start work. I'm on the late shift. I can't wear the same dress to both, can I? Can I, Dad? Dad? Dad!' She shook Frank's shoulders from his daze.

'What?'

'Dad, what is it? What are you thinking about?'

'I need to go in the loft, hen.'

'The loft?'

'Aye. But I don't know...I mean...I can't... remember...what for.' Jackie frowned, and then a smile spread across her face, lighting up her freckles like stars.

'Aww, Dad, I never even thought of that! That's a

really lovely idea! I wonder if it will fit her? Was I about the same age? I bet my mum will have had it all cleaned and wrapped up.'

'She always washed, dried and ironed everything before it went in the loft,' Frank muttered, absentmindedly.

Jackie took the cups and plate into the kitchen. 'I wonder what else is wrapped up?' she shouted back, 'My wee bonnet? Booties?'

Frank opened his eyes wide and nodded. 'Aye. The wee bonnet will be there. So will the booties. And the...your...christening robe!' Frank sprung out of his chair. 'No time like the present!' he said, brightly.

'What? You're going up in the loft now? At this time? No, no, no....you'll wake the wean. Leave it till the weekend. I'm doing the dinner now anyway. Sit down, Dad. Watch the holiday programme.'

'Are you sure? Do you not want to see the gown now?'

'I do, but let's get it at the weekend.'

'If you say so. What are you making?'

'There's not much in. Fried egg and chips, it looks like. Will that do you?'

'That will do me fine, hen.'

Frank sat back and waited for his dinner.

'The sun is shining brightly, it's hot, and the

# Frank

Blackpool beach is buzzing with bathers!' grinned Judith Chalmers from the television. 'I'd better find my space and top up my tan! Good night!'

Frank remembered when he and June took the bus to Blackpool to see the Illuminations, before Jackie was born. Maybe he'd go back one day, take Jackie and the baby. He wondered why June had appeared fainter than before.

'She must be busy up there.' Frank closed his eyes to the sound of Jackie slicing potatoes for chips.

# TROUBLE

'DAD! WHAT ARE YOU DOING GOING UP THERE NOW? THAT'S YOUR GOOD SUIT!' Jackie was standing at the bottom of the steps to the loft, looking up at Frank. He had been acting strangely lately, distant, and made the crazy decision to climb up into the rarely-disturbed, dusty loft in his best suit, just as they were due to leave for Viv's party.

'TAKE ME TWO MINUTES!' shouted Frank, climbing higher and yanking on the old string light.

Jackie checked her painted blue nails and brushed down her new trousers. She was dressed in an electric blue jump suit, electric blue shoes, electric blue bag, electric blue eye shadow and the new *True Blue* mascara, an Avon sample from Viv. Her hair was backcombed with one electric blue slide comb holding back one side of her hair, which was crimped and hair-sprayed into a solid triangle shape. She wore electric blue beads, matching earrings and bead bracelet. She was delighted with what she had picked up in the market, two outfits and all the matching jewellery and a bargain at the shoe stall. The outfits were virtually identical, except the other was a luminous green colour and had a skirt rather than trousers. She planned to wear that one to the christening. The baby was happy downstairs in the arms of Mrs Morrisson, playing with her pull-along phone-on-wheels. She was rolling the wheels back and forth, laughing at the moving eyes. Jackie, anxious to leave before her bedtime, could hear baby June gurgle and Mrs Morrisson talk sweetly to her. She had maybe ten more minutes before the night-time routine began, and she didn't want to be here to listen to any tears.

'Don't you dare get dust on that suit!' she shouted up to the loft, worrying for the suit.

'Yes, dear!' he shouted back, mumbling, 'just like your mother.' He tossed labelled bin bags left and right, searching for the correct one. Frank couldn't believe the amount of bags she had stored.

'Might be worth something, some day!' she'd say, or, 'That's a classic now!'

Here were Jackie's old baby clothes, some old toys, a potty, and a baby walker. He used one finger and thumb to separate the bags covered in soot. He felt a warm surge of familiarity pass through him when he saw her handwriting on the labels. That unmistakable faint June scrawl: *'potty'*, *'baby clothes, 0-6 months'*. He paused to examine every curl of an 'a' or an 'e', the half 's' or unusual 'h' with a flick at the top. Her writing was tiny, and each letter was as thin as a spider leg. To see it again was to feel her close.

Then he spotted it, hanging from the beam.

'CHRISTENING ROBE'. It was written in capitals in a thicker pen. He laughed and shook his head. Even in death, he knew he was being told off - he always needed a push to find anything.

'It's in the fridge!' she'd shout.

'Where? I can't see it!' he'd shout back, staring at the shelves.

'Well, it won't bloody jump out at you, Frank!'

Whatever the 'thing' was, he couldn't ever find it, and in the end, she'd have to come into the kitchen and show him it was just behind the cheese or under the butter.

'CHRISTENING ROBE'.

It hung there like the king of the loft, the rest of its bin-bagged subjects worshipping from the floor. Frank thought that she might as well have written 'IT'S RIGHT HERE IN FRONT OF YOUR FACE'.

He gingerly removed the hanger from the nail, then climbed backwards down the stairs, pulling on the string to put the light out.

'I've got it!' he said, halfway down, 'Jackie, I found it!'

'You pick your moments! We need to leave in a minute!'

# Frank

'You said to get it at the weekend!' he replied, sliding the loft ladders back up. He turned and took a picture off the wall and hung the coathanger on the nail.

'Your fingers are filthy!' she cried.

'Never mind that! There!' He put his arms out as if performing a magic trick, 'Ta da!' Jackie looked at the label. She was suddenly keen to see it. 'Will we open it?'

'Aye, go on then, might as well!' replied Jackie, rolling plastic beads up and down her wrist. Frank carefully removed the bin bag, being sure not to disturb the label and tear June's handwriting or touch the white garment with sooty fingers. There, enclosed in clear film, gleamed Jackie's satin christening robe. It was brighter than bright, with a shine of one of those new kitchen floors off a Flash advert.

Jackie's manicured nails admired the vintage lace that delicately graced the outer trim of the gown, hinting at years gone by and photos of old. Knitted booties with satin ribbon and a matching satin hat were tied around the hanger under the plastic. It was as immaculate as skin after a Sunday scrub.

'Oh, my God, Mum... I won't even need to iron it!' Jackie gasped, one hand over her mouth.

Jackie and Frank stood in silence, and his dusty

hand reached for her manicured fingers. They held hands and stared at the robe, breathing in a mixed moment that dotted husband to wife, father to daughter, mother to daughter and June to June, in a perfect square. Jackie recognised it as such a lovely feeling, a special family moment. She held back a tear. The tear on the way up was happy, but the tear on the way down was sad, and it fell from her cheek to her chest. Her feelings of closeness to her mother were always temporary. She felt her grief like a cancerous lump. The only way to deal with it was to accept it, head on. Tears were her chemo; tears with the tap on. Her sadness was a sore, sickening process of never-ending 'missing'.

Silently, like raindrops racing on a windscreen, droplets rolled down Jackie's cheeks leaving bright blue mascara tracks. Frank wasn't crying. He felt the pride of a lion that had won the hunt.

'What a beautiful wee frock!' he sighed, quietly. 'Still as new as when you wore it!' He noticed Jackie's rolling blue tears.

'Oh, no, no, no, hen. That's enough of that. Come here now.' Frank pulled her in for a cuddle.

'No - your hands are getting me all dirty!'

'C'mon, we'll wash my hands and your face.' He walked Jackie into the bathroom and she looked at her face in the mirror.

# Frank

'What are we like, eh? Look at the state of us!' Frank held his soot-covered hands over the sink while Jackie turned the tap on. They washed face and hands together. Jackie dried her face and reapplied her make-up and mascara, while Frank dabbed at his suit with a corner of wet towel. They kissed baby June good night, thanked the stalwart Mrs Morrisson and set off, to face life once again.

The dance floor wasn't busy so Viv asked the DJ to play *West End Girls* by the Pet Shop Boys. She looked around for her friend and couldn't see her, but spied a boy she didn't recognise. He was slim with a mop of bleached blond curly hair, black at the roots and wearing a jumper that he had pulled down over his fingers. He was standing on his own.

'Aye, right, who are you?' she demanded, walking over, 'In for the free flan?'

'I'm with Jackie!' he replied nervously, flashing a row of perfectly straight white teeth, which impressed Viv. 'I'm Daniel.'

'Oh right! She told me about you, Danny boy!' Viv said, poking him playfully in the chest.

'It's...just...Daniel,' he said, correcting her.

'What are you staring at?' she asked. 'Have I got something in my eye?' She lifted a finger to her eye lid and checked. 'Is it a loose eyelash?'

'No. I like your eye make-up. I like the colours. Is it lilac?' He wanted to endear himself to Jackie's friends, but he barely knew how to talk to Jackie.

'Aye! It is a new shade. How come you know so much about make-up?'

'My mum wears it!' he nodded, keenly.

Viv smiled. It looked as if Daniel was wearing eyeliner under all that hair but it was his thick black lashes, unfair on a boy, should be for girls, she thought.

'Well, tell your mum to come and talk to me! I sell make-up and do Avon parties. If she wants to have an Avon party, I can sort that for her! Or you, if you like that kind of thing?' she laughed.

'Sounds great!' Daniel fidgeted with his jumper sleeve. 'I will tell her!'

'Did you not bring a pal -'

'HAPPY BIRTHDAY TO YOOO!' a voice sang, and Viv swung round to see Jackie hurling towards her, looking very blue and carrying a large rectangular present, wrapped in Happy Birthday paper. Frank strode along behind.

'Wow! You look...BLUE, mate! Maybe we should ask for *Electric Dreams*!' They hugged.

'Shut it, you, ha ha ha!' laughed Jackie, holding Viv by the shoulders to look at her. 'You look amazing! Is that from the market?'

'Aye, it is!'

'I saw that!'

'Did you? No way!'

'I nearly got it! But I got this instead!'

'IT'S BLUETIFUL!' shouted Viv, throwing her head right back and cackling loudly, wheezing like a dog's broken squeaky bone.

'Many happy returns to you, Viv, hen,' offered Frank. 'Who's this?'

'Oh, Jackie! Daniel is here! Look!'

'I saw that! Hiya, Daniel, how are you? Dad, this is Daniel. Daniel, this is my dad. He can call you Frank, right, Dad?'

'Aye, that's fine. How are you doing, son?' Frank extended his hand and Daniel pushed his sleeve up and took it.

'Good, thank you, Mister...'

'Frank,' he said, nodding once. 'Right then! What are we all having?'

'I'll have a vodka, please, Frank.'

'Same for me, please, Dad.'

'Pint of lager, please, Mister -'

'Frank, son. Just Frank. Please, call me Frank. Right, I'll get them in!' Frank walked off to the bar.

'First drink's free!' called Viv.

'Oh, ya beauty! That's my round sorted!' winked Frank.

'Do you need a hand?' offered Daniel.

'No, son - I'll get a tray,' he called back, 'You get a table.'

They sat down at the nearest table and Jackie gave Viv her birthday present.

'I hope you like it!'

'Oh... will I open it now or later?'

'Open it now!' Jackie clapped. Viv tore open the paper to reveal a white box. On the other side, written in large letters were the words *SODA STREAM*. Jackie knew Viv was desperate for a fizzy drinks maker after she found out it made different colas from flavoured syrups. Viv hadn't stopped talking about it for months. Jackie had to put aside a little bit of her wages every week to afford this little luxury, but it was worth it to see Viv's face, and it seemed that everybody was getting one these days.

'*Get busy with the fizz-eh!*' sang Jackie. 'There's limeade, orangeade, cherryade, you name it!'

'Soda Stream! Oh, Jackie!' replied Viv, stroking the box. 'How did you afford this? I really wanted one of these.'

'Now you can have that green tongue any time you like!'

'Jackie - this is too much.'

'Now, now, no, it isn't. Just a wee thank you. For

all your help. You know.' They exchanged a glance that sealed their bond.

'You're the best.' Viv leaned in for a hug, then took the Soda Stream over to her mum's table to show her. Her mum waved over at Jackie and gave an impressed 'wow' face. Her dad smiled and gave a thumbs up. His leg rested up on another chair. Frank returned with the drinks.

'Here we go. There you are, son. That's yours, Jackie. I got a Cola for you to share across the two vodkas.'

'Lovely, thanks, Dad.'

Outside on the stairs, Tommy Fletcher smoked a cigarette, taking the last two puffs, followed by an immediate inhale.

'I don't know why you want to go. We're not invited!' Maureen checked her face in her compact mirror and shivered. 'Why don't we go round to the Black Dog? There won't be anybody there and we can have a quiet drink and a canoodle.' Maureen's pleas were not heard. Tommy flicked his cigarette away, aiming it at a nearby puddle. He listened for the 'hiss' as it hit the water. He liked that sound.

'No,' he said, removing a comb from his inside pocket and combing over a Brylcreem parting, one side, and then the other. 'We're going in.' He pushed the double door and strode through the short corridor, before opening the other door, and pausing to look back at Maureen. 'I want to see exactly who it is she's running about with now.'

'But, Tommy...why would you -' Maureen tried to enquire as to why he would care, but he was off, through the door.

Bobby the barman spotted him immediately and scooted out from behind the bar and over to Tommy.

'I don't want any trouble now, Tommy, you hear? This is a party.' Tommy put his hands up.

'You'll get no trouble from me, Bobby. Just in for a quiet pint. Isn't that right, Maureen?' Maureen looked back at him, blankly. Seeing Maureen was with him, Bobby relented, reluctantly.

'Okay, but just stay over by the side of the bar...'

'You won't even know I'm here. Right, Maureen?' Maureen nodded, her thin lips turned down at the corners. They did as directed and stood at the right hand side of the bar. Jackie noticed his entrance and held his stare. He was looking at her while he gulped down the two whiskies he had ordered. Maureen had thought that one was for her.

'Another two halves here, Bobby.'

'And I'll have a voddie and coke, please, Bobby,' said Maureen, nervously.

# Frank

'Be with you in a second.' Bobby finished pulling a pint, took the money and rung it up in the till.

'Get your purse out, then!' Tommy motioned to Maureen's bag. He turned to look around. Jackie was here, chatting to her friend Viv and what looked like a Uni student. Tommy hated students. He watched him as he flicked his hair around his face and Jackie laughed. Jackie was looking fantastic. She had gained a little bit of weight and looked young and fresh, like when he first met her... before she...complicated things. Just as he was looking at her legs, she caught his glance - then she quickly looked away. Tommy felt sure there was a flicker of something. A smile or a look...something. He threw back his whisky.

Jackie grabbed Viv by the arm and pulled her in the direction of the Ladies.

'He's here! Tommy's here!'

'I know. There's nothing we can do about it, Jackie. It's not a private function, it's open to the public as well. Look, just stay out of his road, okay?'

'Okay.'

'He's just out to rile you. Don't give him the satisfaction. He must be bored of that Maureen. Did you see the state of her? You look amazing next to her. He'll be gutted. Too bad. Too little, too late!'

'You're dead right, Viv.' Jackie turned to the

mirror. She fumbled through her bag and pulled out a Pink Fizz lipstick. She applied the lipstick and flashed Viv a smile in the mirror. Leaving the toilets arm in arm, they grabbed Daniel and marched him to the dance floor. Daniel loved being with the girls but felt a little embarrassed to dance. He fiddled with his hair, pulling it across his face like curtains.

Jackie danced, stealing glances at Tommy, who stared right back at her. He raised his eyebrows as she looked over, letting her know that he approved.

Trouble.

June was very faint. She had appeared in Jackie's chair while Jackie danced.

Trouble.

Frank could barely make out what she was saying. She faded away almost immediately as a bar stool swooped past where she sat. It was aimed at the dance floor.

# YES, DEAR

The bar stool landed off the mark but was enough to part the crowd. Tommy marched over to Daniel and his spit landed like a bullet on the toe of Daniel's High Tops. He was ready to punch the student's lights out, with his stupid hair and baggy jumper. Lunging towards Daniel, his knuckles felt hard as they brushed against his suit jacket pockets.

Daniel put his hands up, fingers wide. 'Look, mate, I don't want any trouble here. I was invited.'

'Answer me one question, are you with her?' Tommy pointed to Jackie, whilst keeping his gaze on Daniel. Jackie shook her head. 'Answer me.'

'We're just friends,' Daniel protested.

'Well, then, what are you doing dancing with her? Right in front of my face?' He began pacing Daniel in a circle, poking his shoulders and chest, punctuating each word. 'Let me tell you this. She. Belongs. To me!'

'Tommy, leave it, please,' pleaded Jackie. 'He's just my pal from work... we're only dancing. That's all. There's three of us here, dancing together.'

Daniel was frightened. He knew about Tommy but didn't know he was this violent.

'It's my birthday and you're not invited,' Viv interjected, squaring up to Tommy, hands on hips.

'You can't stop me coming into a public bar, doll!' He waved his arm around to all the spectators. 'And I'm not here to join your crap excuse for a party, I'm here for Jackie. Don't tell me you weren't looking over, because I saw you. I saw you looking at me, Jackie. I think we both know it's time to take you home.' Tommy was definitive in his statement, one part warning, one part invitation; the way he always used to talk to her.

'Home? I live with my dad, after you chucked us out. And that's where I'm staying.'

'You left! I never chucked you out!'

'Aye, you did, you liar!' shouted Viv.

'Oh, don't worry, he did us a favour, Viv.' Jackie looked down at her nails.

Tommy leaned in closely towards her, and lifted her chin. He spoke quietly enough that only she could hear.

'I saw you looking at me. I know we still have something. Don't deny yourself another chance with me, Jackie. We belong together. You know it and I know it. You need me.' He moved his hands to her shoulders and stroked up and down her arms.

Jackie looked into his eyes, her heart and head now in battle. For months, she had managed to cope; to harden her heart, block him out, but her forgotten loneliness was awake to his tender touch. Behind the bad boy, there was a gentleness she'd once loved, wasn't there? Or was it one-sided love? She did love him, but could he ever love her back? Could she fall asleep on his shoulder on the bus? Would they laugh when he threw the baby in the air? Take her to the swings? Play with the plastic animals? Would he be there for Jackie at three o'clock in the morning if she needed him? Would he be asleep beside her? A familiar shape to reach out and touch?

Or would the pillow be empty; dented in the centre, like their love.

She searched his face; this was not love between them, she thought, not the same love as her mum and dad used to have for each other. Not the love that takes tumbles and turns, tolerates, endures, fights, makes up, grows old and grows deep. That 'Yes, dear' love. When parents didn't even agree, but still said, 'Yes, dear' to keep the peace. There for each other; a constant. Jackie's love for Tommy was a fleeting loneliness, and that's why a life with him could never work. He reminded her of how alone she felt, even when they were together. Pretending to be happy, like life was a play.

Viv interrupted her thoughts.

'Take your hands off her, man, you don't own her. She's not your property! Jackie, you're not his property!'

'Get off me, you stupid bitch!' shouted Tommy, his hands still on Jackie's shoulders. Jackie, aware of what was happening, remained frozen inside her sadness.

Frank watched with the others. He didn't know what to do. Somebody was going to get hurt and his daughter was right at the centre. He felt his age, a useless age! As a younger man, he'd have dived in, but now he'd throw a punch and crack a hip.

June wasn't here to advise. He kept looking for her in the other chair, but she didn't appear. He'd have to make this decision by himself. Say something and hope not to feel a thump. Deciding to try the sensible approach, he stood up from the table and quietly and purposefully approached the shouting huddle on the dance floor.

'Excuse me, now, Tommy. We don't want any trouble. Why don't you be on your way, son,' Frank offered, cautiously.

'Ha ha ha! You think you can take me, Frank McNeill? Me? Square-go with Granda? Stay out of my way, old man!' Tommy gave a Frank a hard push and he fell backwards into a table. Jackie snapped out of her trance and moved quickly to stand between her dad and Tommy while Viv and a few other party guests rushed to Frank's aid.

'Don't you dare touch my dad! You lay a finger on him again and I'll slice you in your sleep!'

'In my sleep? Ah!' Tommy brushed his shoulders, 'So she's coming home with me, after all!' he announced. 'Good girl.'

Jackie noticed Maureen alone at the bar.

'Why don't you just leave, Tommy. You're not welcome here. Just go. Take your girlfriend with you. Poor girl, no doubt wondering what she's doing with you. He's a low life, sweetheart. Don't waste your time with him,' she shouted to Maureen.

'Her?' Tommy pointed at Maureen. 'Forget about her. She was just something to keep me warm at night while you were away. As if. The state of that.' Maureen burst into floods of tears.

'YOU SAID... I WAS... YOUR TEA CAKE!' she sobbed, rushing off to the toilet, hiding her face. Bobby forgot himself for a second and ran into the toilet after her, leaving the bar unattended.

'CUT THE MUSIC,' he shouted to the DJ as the Ladies door closed slowly behind them. The DJ nervously scratched Bow Wow Wow's *Go Wild In The Country* off half way through.

Viv's dad managed to find his feet, limped in behind the bar and began to quietly pour himself a pint. His wife tutted, rolled her eyes and mouthed, 'Get me a good gin.' He waggled his finger at others who wanted a drink, telling them to wait a minute.

'We're finished, Tommy,' said Jackie. 'We finished when you looked the wrong way. When you didn't like my "mess" in your flat. When this pregnant girlfriend wasn't convenient for you. You didn't love me when I was knee deep in nappies and washing. You were all too quick to remind me that my hair wasn't as bouncy as it used to be. I was a mug! You had me on a string. How many strings you dangling, now, Tommy? You might think you want me tonight, but for how long? Not long, I can assure you of that! I'd be back out the door before long, you can bet on it.'

'We can do it, Jackie, make it work. You, me and your wee girl; if it's mine. Maybe even until we're old and grey, if we're lucky.' He raised his eyebrows and nodded.

'*If it's yours*? Do you even know her name? You can't just turn up months later, demanding me back! No way. Get lost! You disgust me.'

Jackie turned to walk away towards her dad.

'Is that so? Well, what about this wee dick?' Tommy gave Daniel a sideways poke. 'Is he your new squeeze? Is he? I've a right to know!' Keeping his wild gaze fixed on Jackie, Tommy swung round and punched Daniel squarely on the nose. Daniel, whose hands were trembling, raised his palms towards his nose. Blood poured through his fingers. Viv screamed. This triggered a wall of screaming from other women who had been watching. Some people scrambled towards the door. One of them shouted, 'Happy Birthday, Viv!' as they rushed out.

Viv jumped on Tommy's back.

'Oh, Viv, no!' gasped her mum, hands to her mouth.

'I thought you liked a good fight?' replied Viv's dad, pouring another pint. 'Our Viv can handle herself. This is what happens at a good party.' He flexed his arm muscle. 'Look at her there ... raised by a wolf, she was.' His wife nodded proudly and sipped her more expensive gin.

'HIT ME BACK! COME ON! WELL, GO ON THEN!' Viv's rage raced through her body, pulsing every muscle like a prize fighter.

'LEAVE IT!' screamed Jackie. 'PLEASE!'

Tommy pushed past Daniel, knocking him over, then kicked the swing entrance doors so that they slammed up against the wall.

'Och, naw!' complained Viv's dad. He pushed a glass up to the brandy optic.

'He might come back,' muttered Viv's mum.

'Here, take that to Frank, he'll need it,' he

instructed his wife. She walked to Frank and placed the brandy beside him, asking if he was okay.

Jackie rushed to her dad and put her arms around him.

'Are you all right, Dad?'

'Aye, I'm fine, hen, I'm fine. Do you think that's him gone?'

'I don't know. I hope so. I hope poor Daniel will be all right.'

Viv saw the brandy and took a gulp. 'He won't be back. Daniel was lucky it was just his nose,' she said. 'Could have been worse if I hadn't jumped in. Could have been a lot worse. But don't you worry, I'm ready for him.' She necked the rest of the brandy. Daniel approached the table, holding his nose.

'The police are outside. They want to talk to me about Tommy. I'm sorry about your party, Viv.'

'Not your fault! I'll come outside with you and talk to them as well.'

'I'm sorry too, Viv. I didn't know he was going to turn up,' said Jackie.

'Why are you sorry? It was magic!' Viv smiled and Frank shook his head.

'What about all your presents and the clearing up?'

'My mum and dad will do that, don't worry. I'll

phone you later. Better go.' Viv hugged Jackie. Daniel gave a little wave. Jackie waved back and watched them walk outside to the flashing light.

The door of the Ladies opened and Bobby appeared with his arm around Maureen, still comforting her.

'C'mon, we'll get you a drink. Vodka, is it?'

'Mmm hmm,' replied Maureen, through sniffs.

'What the he- GET OUT FROM THERE!' Bobby shouted to Viv's dad. He tried to scramble back through the hatch of the bar, but held his leg and began limping again.

'I was just looking for a pen,' he said. 'For the police.'

Bobby guided Maureen onto a stool.

Frank turned to Jackie. 'Let's go home, hen,' he said. Jackie took her dad's arm.

'Yes, dear,' she smiled.

They took the ten-minute walk home through the town past the shops. Neither said a word. Neither felt the drizzle. They just walked.

Mrs Morrisson was asleep in the chair with her mouth open. The TV was off. All the toys had been tidied into the box and the dishes were done. Jackie sent her dad to bed and walked Mrs Morrisson four doors down to her house. She walked back and locked the back door. Feeling shaken, she made a cup of tea, then drank it while thinking about the washing she forgot to bring in, still out on the line. She hoped it would be dry by the morning; that the rain would go off. The grass needed cutting, too. Another thing her dad forgot to do. She put the cup in the sink and walked to the hall. She gently removed her new shoes and placed them carefully under the stairs. She switched out the hall light and walked up the stairs, her stockinged feet brushing the soft carpet, cramped toes stretching out like tree branches in spring. She looked in on her dad as he slept on his side. His slippers lay on the floor, side-by-side, ready for the morning. She marvelled at how he never rolled onto her mum's side of the bed, even though she wasn't there. His face was a map of lines, and yet, although he was older, she somehow felt maternal towards him. She stroked his head once. He was sleeping deeply, but not snoring. She left his room and looked into her own. Baby June was asleep in her cot. She looked just like him, on her side, cheek squashed against the brightly striped sheet. A circle of drool darkened a few of the coloured stripes. Jackie put her hand on the baby's heart, something she did every night, to feel her chest move up and down. She thought about Tommy and the trouble he caused.

'We don't need him,' she whispered.

# Frank

She felt ready to go to bed. She took off her bracelets and earrings and placed them one by one on the bedside table, lay down on her bed, thinking she'd brush her teeth in a second, get pyjamas on in a minute, un-tuck the blankets in a minute...She felt herself drifting in her good clothes, and hoped they wouldn't be too wrinkled in the morning.

# THE KISS

Frank was awake before his eyes opened. He stretched out to momentarily feel for June. Another dream. This time, she stood in the distance, waving. He tried to reach for her but she was too far away. He called but she couldn't hear him. His feet were stuck in something heavy like syrup, holding him in the same spot. He felt he must have been shouting in his sleep for sure as it was so vivid and pained and he felt exhausted. Sluggishly, he rolled onto his side and slid his feet straight into his slippers. He rubbed his eyes and made his way out of bed.

The house was unusually quiet. He poked his head around the door of Jackie's room and a glorious sight woke his heart. She was holding the baby in her arms as she looked through the lace curtain to the street, probably at nothing in particular, but the way she held her baby close in the morning light reminded him of how June used to hold Jackie. Standing, rocking her quietly, humming half a tune. The baby's hand was buried deep in her mother's morning hair, her fingers exploring the tangles. In a mirror image, Jackie's hand cradled the soft part of baby June's scalp. Contentedly, she nuzzled a sleepy face into her mother's neck. A beam of light shone through the curtain and haloed their heads. Frank drew breath. He knew, or at least he felt, this was June's doing. He took comfort that she was watching his girls, guiding Jackie along the path of motherhood.

Frank had become accustomed to attributing all small good fortunes to June. If he lost his glasses in the kitchen, then found them again by the bed, or put on a pair of trousers and found a few pounds for a pint, he'd say it was down to June. He felt sure he was going to see her soon, maybe today.

'Cup of tea, hen?' he whispered.

'Oh, that would be nice, thanks, Dad.' Baby June popped up her head at the sound of another voice.

'Good morning, sunshine,' said Frank. 'Look at her, she's so good in the mornings. You're so good in the mornings! Such a good-natured wee thing, she is.'

'Daaa!' replied the baby, quietly. 'Gaaaa.'

'Granda!' replied Frank. 'Granda, Granda, Granda, Granda, Granda!' he repeated, walking towards her, stopping right in front of her with a light tap on her nose. 'Granda's got to make the tea! Did you get up and get dressed already, Jackie? Your make-up's needing a wee sort out, hen.'

'Aye, right, very funny, very good. I fell asleep in my clothes, as I'm sure you guessed.'

'Well, I'm not surprised. Not surprised at all. What a night. Some night! That bloody Tommy!'

'I hope that's the last we see of him.'

'Me too, hen.' He shook his head and left the room to head downstairs. 'I'll get the toast on - have we any bread?'

'Check the bread bin. There might be a few slices.'

Frank felt his left knee creak and crack as he took the stairs, carefully holding onto the bannister. Making his way into the kitchen, he flicked the kettle on and removed two cups from the cupboard and two teabags from the box.

'Needing what?' he said to himself, and to Jackie if she could hear him. He stood by the kettle. 'Oh, aye. Toast!' he said, opening the bread bin. There were three slices left. 'Only three slices.'

`Bread in the freezer,` he heard.

'What?'

`Bread in the freezer.`

'June? Where are you? I can't -'

'Dad. It's me. It's just me. Did you mean, "Jackie"?' Jackie stood, now wearing her pyjamas and dressing gown, a concerned look on her face.

'No, I meant your mum! Did you just tell me there was bread in the freezer?'

'No. I said to check the bread bin.'

'Aye. That's what I thought, but...' Frank opened the freezer door and there was a loaf of bread inside. He pulled out half the slices and left the rest in there. 'How many slices are you wanting?'

'Two for me, and make two for the baby cos she won't eat the crusts...but Dad...were you talking to yourself?'

'Of course I was. I'm blinking well nearly seventy. Will I make boiled eggs?'

'Aye, okay. Make the baby's soft so she can dip her soldiers! You want wee soldiers? Yes, you do!'

Jackie went to put baby June in her high chair as Frank boiled three eggs. He looked around the kitchen, unlocked and opened the back door, looked outside, then closed it again. He looked behind the door and had a quick look to see if she was sitting on the couch. The eggs bubbled. The toast popped. He spread butter and sliced into soldiers. He took the toast to the high chair, all the while looking around and behind.

Jackie slid a VHS of *Thomas* into the video recorder and turned on the television.

'Are you seeing her again, Dad?'

'Eh? Don't be daft. I've never seen her. How? Have you seen her?' he asked, more hopeful than he cared to reveal.

'No. I miss her but I don't see her.' Frank

retreated to the kitchen to drain the eggs. 'Dad?'

'Aye, hen?'

'What are we going to do about... Tommy?'

Frank sliced the top off the egg and the yolk spilled over the sides down the shell and onto the eggcup. He moved it onto a plastic plate and took it in to the highchair. Baby June was looking at the television. Thomas The Tank Engine's big blue face filled the screen as the music played.

'I don't know, Jackie, I really don't. Is his mum or dad about?'

'His mum lives in Birmingham. He never talked about his dad. I don't even know if he's got a dad.'

'Well, we'd better just hope that's it, then. He won't come back. He's never been round here, not to this house, anyway.' Frank and Jackie picked up their teas, toast and eggs from the kitchen and sat on the couch and chair, high chair in between.

'Fat Controller looks like Father Cleary!'

'Ha ha! So he does! Just needs a top hat!'

'Ha ha ha! The belly!'

'Dad! It's Sunday! You told the Father we'd be at Mass!'

'Oh, buck! What time is it?'

'Ten o'clock.'

'Right. We'll go to twelve Mass.'

'I need to sort my hair out!'

'Aye, you're right there!' he smiled. 'I need to sort mine out as well.' Frank patted at his bald patch.

'Which one?'

'The one at the front. I need your hairspray.' They both laughed lightly. Jackie tossed her half-eaten toast down to the plate on the arm of the couch and dashed off to wash her hair.

Frank continued to watch *Thomas* with baby June. The story was of a grumpy-faced engine named Diesel who had been naughty and was told to wait in the tunnel. Frank cleared away the plates and again, checked around while he tidied. Not sure where to look or what he was looking for, he even had a look in the cupboard under the stairs.

Once all ready for Mass, just as they were about to leave at 11.30 on the dot, baby June vomited her egg all over Jackie's blouse. She decided it best they stay at home as the baby was sick, so Frank set off on his own. Arriving at Mass, he took his pamphlet and hymnbook and sat roughly ten rows from the front on the far left, where he used to sit with June. He nodded to old Mary sitting two rows in front of him. Her curled white hair was in its usual style of a cloud.

The priest's voice boomed, 'Hymn number 432. Four-three-two.' The organist began to play. Frank recognised it immediately as a nice hymn, and began to sing along.

*I, the Lord of sea and sky,*
*I have heard My people cry.*
*All who dwell in dark and sin,*
*My hand will save.*

*I who made the stars of night,*
*I will make their darkness bright.*
*Who will bear My light to them?*
*Whom shall I send?*

*Here I am Lord, It is I, Lord,*
*I have heard You calling in the night.*
*I will go Lord, if You lead me.*
*I will hold Your people in my heart.*

As he reached the chorus, he realised he was unable to sing any more and instantly fell quiet. He had been singing the first verse fine but it was the chorus that choked him up; it was one of June's funeral hymns. Without control, he began to sob quietly through the rest of the singing. No-one noticed, as people rarely looked left or right in church, and certainly never behind. He looked up to the roof, but was not sure why. He looked back ahead, wiped tears with his handkerchief and pretended to clean his glasses.

He was silent for the rest of Mass, going through the motions of standing up, sitting and kneeling, saying *Our Father* and taking communion but not really present or engaged in any of it.

He exited out the back door and joined the queue to shake Father Cleary's hand. Jackie had told him that he 'needed to be seen' for her to get the baby christened.

'Hello, Frank. Could you wait for me back inside, please?'

'Yes, Father.' Frank was once an altar boy and had never been anything other than obedient as far as priests were concerned, considering he thought some of them could be quite scary.

'Through this way.' Father Cleary walked through in his sandals, robes flowing behind him, confident in the knowledge that Frank would follow. They walked through to the back of the church and past an open green door that led into the Church House. They sat down in Father Cleary's office, which doubled as a dining room, with French doors opening to a small garden. The room was very cluttered, with piles of dusty papers on a desk and various old books strewn around, it looked to Frank, in a higgledy-piggledy fashion. There was a dog's bed covered in hair in the corner, but no dog to be seen. A plate of shortbread sat by a few pens on the desk.

'Care for a...'

'No, thanks, Father.'

'Quite right. A minute on the lips!' The priest looked around for a place to put the shortbread but there was no other space for it to sit, so he opened a desk drawer and placed it inside and closed it again before leaning forward across the desk.

'How are you, Frank?'

'I'm fine, aye, good, aye.'

'Good, good. It's nice to see you back with us at Mass... at last.'

'Aye, it took a while, after, you know, the passing of June. Better late than never!' he tried to joke. *The passing of June?* Frank wondered why he had said it so formally.

'June was a great comfort and companion to you. It's natural that you will miss her and perhaps not want to face certain places that remind you...of her passing...like Church, for example. But this is where you have support.'

Frank felt his chin wobble. How did the priest have this effect on him? How did he make him feel like a boy again? He had been in here two minutes and he was ready to say sorry...for something...to break down...somehow, because he'd missed Mass? The priest had brought him to the brink of tears.

'Grief is a very powerful emotion, Frank, but do not fear it; do not be afraid to open the wound. The Lord can be here for you at this time. Lean on our Lord.' Frank had to look down at the fluff on the carpet. He felt a build up inside him, rushing to the top like a volcano about to erupt. 'You are in a safe place, without judgment,' the priest continued, 'there's nobody here. Nobody can hear you but me, and Christ above. If there is something you're holding onto...something you want to speak of...let our Lord offer you comfort.' Again, Frank remained quiet. 'Frank,' the priest said, gently, 'It's amazing, the view from the altar. I can see all the faces. I could see you. Row eleven, left hand side.'

'I can't...'

'Go on...it's all right.'

Words began to rush from Frank's mouth. 'I think I'm going mad, Father! I can see her. I swear I can see her...She even talks to me. She comes... and...and...then she goes. I never know when she's coming back. And she asks me to look for things. And tells me how to blow on my pie. And I keep forgetting stuff, names of things and people. I...I can't remember! I search the places in my brain where I know the answer used to be, and it isn't there! It's not there! Just blank spaces! My brain is full of blank spaces...then she creeps in. She creeps in...to the empty corners and pockets. I can see her! Jackie can't see her. I talk to her and she talks back to me. I can smell her perfume. But she's coming less and less and the last time she was hardly here, then she was gone, then another time, it was just a voice and Father, I don't know what to do...Help me...' The hot teardrops spilled from Frank's eyes like river rapids, his old hankie a useless dam. The priest offered him a box of tissues. He took two.

'I know, Frank. I know. I've been watching you, see. I've seen you talking to her.'

'Oh, my God! Where? Have you? Have other people? Folk are going to think I've gone mental.'

'A few places. The supermarket. No, I'm pretty sure it was just me that saw you. Don't worry, you're quite safe.'

'I don't think I am! I mean, who sees their dead wife? Why, Father? Why am I seeing her? I've heard that sometimes the dead visit but why is she visiting me?'

'Grief is strong. It has power over you that you can't control. Some say it can trick the mind...there are many theories. Some say you see what you want to see, or what you need to see, because you can't let go. I think that there is a deep valley of grief in your heart, Frank. And you've held it there, down in there, like a big pile of clothes that nobody wants to iron, squashed down at the bottom of a basket.'

'I should have helped her...I could have stopped her...I never stopped her drinking...I could have stopped her drinking...I feel guilty because I didn't ...I just let her, I couldn't stop her.' He was sobbing, trying to catch his breath. The priest offered Frank another tissue.

'She had an illness, Frank. Nobody could have stopped her. God had a path for her, and she was chosen. She was a good woman, Frank, a good, kind woman. But she was sick, and sadly it was her time.'

Frank tried to gather himself together. He blew his nose and wiped his eyes, but the tears kept coming. 'I never stopped her...and she died...she died.' He couldn't get a breath.

'You've had so much to contend with since June died, what with the baby and all...you've hardly had a moment to think about this mammoth thing that has happened to you.'

They stayed quiet for a few minutes as Frank wept in his chair. The priest came around the desk and sat on the other chair. As Frank cried, he felt a hand on his shoulder and he could hear the priest mumbling prayers. After he came to the end, he offered Frank another tissue.

'Frank, I want to tell you a story.' Frank looked up, wide-eyed and childlike, ready to be nourished by his words. 'Some weeks after my Granny died, I had a visit from her. She was sitting on the couch. I could see her but nobody else could. I rushed to her and sat on her knee, burying myself in her pillowy softness. I missed her so much. I remember breathing in her talcum smell. I felt her skin, soft and baggy, powdery-white. I said to her, "Granny!" I said, "I thought you had died." And she said, "I did, Pudsey, but I couldn't leave without saying goodbye to you!" And she gave me a kiss on the forehead. It was clear to me that this really happened, I had felt the kiss, even though nobody had seen it. I felt that kiss, and I knew that my Granny had visited me. Maybe it was a trick of the mind, the strength of my grief, maybe it wasn't. But whatever it was, a presence, a visit, a dream, I knew it was special. It was mine to keep. My special Granny had visited me. Frank, what you have described with June's visits...it's the same. It's special. For some, this is grief. Whilst it brings the pain of death, it also brings the joy of life and what life once was, to have been loved, to have felt love, the greatest gift, the first commandment. What you have described is the great power of love.' He paused. 'June must have loved you very much and sometimes...we must keep someone close for a little while...before we can carry on.'

'Is she...a ghost?'

'I don't know, Frank. But if it were me, I wouldn't question it.'

'Will she come again?'

'Well, my feeling is that she will be there when you need her. You will feel her close when you need to. And then one day, suddenly you'll find...you're okay by yourself. You're rebuilt. Try to focus on the good, the now, what you have. Your daughter, your granddaughter. It's life. This is life. Try to look forward. And share in her memory. Celebrate her stories. Nobody expects you to keep them all inside and keep her memory hidden away. Talk about her. You can do that now, can't you? You're the boss of the family now, right?'

Frank smiled. June used to say that she was the boss but he was in charge.

'Father, sometimes I'm frightened. What if I can't remember her - like I can't remember where I put the keys, or...'

'We are all frightened, Frank. Do you not think that our Lord Jesus Christ wasn't petrified at the sight of that cross? Sure he must have been frightened out of his very wits! And sure, he himself knew it was coming! He knew about it before it happened! And he still came back, himself, now, didn't he? Sure I'm sure we all come back one way or another, as something or other, but that's beside the point for now. All we do know is, that death brings hurt; a deep cut, and it's the living that have to carry the burden. I carried the burden of the death of my Granny. And after that visit, I cried for her, I wanted her to come back and see me again. But in time, my burden began to lift, day by day as I let her go, to take her place in Heaven.'

'Did you ever see her again? Did she come back?'

'No, I never saw her again. But I know she's watching me. I know she's there. My mother says I was a very sad little boy that imagined things, but me and my Granny, we know better.' Father Cleary smiled and offered Frank another tissue - which he refused. The priest took the shortbread back out of the drawer. 'Eat one of these. Sugar is good,' he said. 'You have set free a little of what you have held inside, and that's a good thing. Who knows, maybe June will visit you again, or maybe not, but know that you can do this without her. You already are. And if she's visiting you less and less, perhaps you might consider the fact that you're coping...without her.'

Frank fell silent with his thoughts. He politely refused the plate of shortbread again.

'Thank you, Father. I'd better go. Jackie will be wondering where I am. I'm sorry for the...I don't know where it came from.'

The priest nodded. 'Come and see me again soon.'

'I will. Thanks again.' Frank walked outside into the afternoon breeze and pulled his jacket lapels in.

'God bless,' waved the priest. He watched Frank from the doorway until he walked out of sight.

# SHUT THE DOOR

'Fair play to you, Father, you did a beautiful job. That was a lovely service.'

'Thank you, Frank. I ought to know what I'm doing by now!' They laughed together, shuffling alongside a table with paper plates in hand, collecting sausage rolls from the buffet. The trestle table had been borrowed from Mrs Morrisson. It was covered with a tablecloth and it heaved in the middle with vol au vents filled with tuna, meat paste sandwiches, egg mayonnaise sandwiches, ham rolls, potato salad, coleslaw, pickles, beetroot, a quiche, and a hedgehog of hot dogs with pineapple chunks and cheeses. There were crisps, Ritz crackers and a dish of butter beside a loaf of sliced bread. A giant christening cake sat proudly in the middle between two heavy crystal ashtrays filled with peanuts. The priest piled his plate high with hedgehog sticks and crisps.

'Some buffet, this, Frank, eh?' said Viv's dad, limping along behind them, his paper plate buckling with the weight of food.

'This kind lady to thank for that!' He motioned to Mrs Morrisson, who was folding serviettes and ensuring everybody had a knife and fork. 'Make sure you get some yourself, now, Mrs!'

'I will, Frank, in a wee minute.'

Jackie stood with Viv, baby June on her hip, as Viv took pictures with a new camera she'd bought with her birthday money.

'Only four flashes left! We'll have to make sure we get one of all of us.'

'We can do that. I just want to see if Mrs Morrisson is okay. Can you take the baby?'

'Mum, take my camera. I need to take the baby for Jackie.' Viv passed the camera to her mum who was eating, sitting on the couch. 'Come to your favourite auntie, hen! Jackie, she looks so beautiful in her wee hat and gown and booties. I love her name, Jackie, I love it. I didn't know you were going to put a middle name in there.'

'It is. It's a very nice name', said Viv's mum.

'I didn't know I was going to do it either but it felt like the right thing to do.'

She made her way through the friends and neighbours to Mrs Morrisson and gave her a kiss on the cheek.

'I used to know somebody who reminded me of you, Mrs Morrisson. She was a patient on my ward. She was a really kind lady.'

'That's nice, Jackie, what a lovely thing to say.

Have you had something to eat? Get a plate now, hen, while there's some left.'

'Did you hear the service, the baby's name?'

'Well, you see, Jackie, I had to leave to set up the buffet so I was only there at the start, you see, and I missed *What name do you give your child?* and that's the bit I wanted to see but, you know, Frank had given me a key to the house to set up and I wanted to have it all nice for you. But June is a lovely name, so it is, and your mum would be so proud of you and you, yourself, look beautiful-'

'I gave the baby a middle name too, Mrs Morrisson.'

'Did you now? Ah, isn't that nice now, a middle name, eh? Very posh!'

'Do you want to know what her middle name is?'

'Of course I do.'

'It's Patricia. Do you like it?'

'Oh, Jackie, now! Oh! Jackie! But that's my-'

'I know it's your first name, Mrs Morrisson. And I wanted to name her after you as well. I think my mum would have liked that.'

'Oh, Jackie, that's lovely, thank you. You're an angel.' She hugged Jackie, then handed her a plate. 'Now, if your mum was here, she'd say that you must eat, Jackie, before this greedy lot scoff it all. Here! Frank! Let me give you a hand with that!' Mrs

# Frank

Morrisson moved over to help Frank pour out halves of whisky into small glasses. 'You have a lovely daughter, Frank. You're very lucky.'

'I know.'

'I only wish my son was like her.'

'I never knew you had a son, Mrs!'

'I have a son in Linlithgow, you remember, the tea towel? But he never comes to visit.'

'That's a shame. I'm sorry to hear that.'

'Ah, don't be. People have to live their own lives, don't they?' Mrs Morrisson moved away to hand out a few more plates. Everything made sense to Frank now. The casseroles, the offers to babysit. He pulled Jackie to one side.

'What is it, Dad?'

'Did you know Mrs Morrisson had a son in Linlithgow?'

'No?' She bit into a vol au vent.

'She said he never comes to see her. I think she's lonely.'

Jackie noticed something in her dad's eyes; she put the remaining pastry down onto her plate.

'Dad.'

'Yes?'

'Is this you realising that Mrs Morrisson isn't after you?'

'What? Don't be ridiculous!' Frank pulled his

stomach in, put his shoulders back, and looked over at Mrs Morrisson. 'I just feel sorry for the woman!'

'She's just a nice wee woman, Dad. That's all it is.'

'I know that!' Frank replied, indignantly.

'Her son is an idiot. It's his loss. She's a wonderful woman.' Frank and Jackie looked over to Mrs Morrisson pouring drinks. He felt bad for all the times he had avoided her on the bus and hadn't listened to her stories, so wrapped up in his own.

'We should include her more, Jackie. Maybe she can iron my shirts or something.'

'Include her by ironing your shirts?' Jackie sighed. 'For goodness sake, Dad, you take the biscuit.' She laughed and shook her head, put her plate down and went back to take baby June from Viv. 'Now then, June Patricia, let's get you a wee bite to eat, eh?' She untied the baby's satin hat and flattened down her fluffy hair.

The doorbell rang. Jackie looked around but nobody else seemed to register a noise. Viv's mum continued eating. Viv had moved in behind the glass door of the hi-fi and was flicking through records. Everybody else was chatting. Jackie sighed and carried the baby to the door. She opened it to be greeted by the hopeful face of Bobby, the Workmen's barman. Standing beside him was Maureen, Tommy's ex. She was carrying a huge parcel with a pink bow.

'Hi, Jackie...hope it's okay...your dad invited us... well, me...and a friend...you remember Maureen?'

'Hi, Jackie. Nice to see you.' Maureen held out the gift.

'I know that Maureen might be the last person you want to see today...'

'...or the second last,' added Maureen.

'...but, well, let's just say things have moved on, and Maureen is, well, should I say it, Maureen?'

'Of course you should say it!' Maureen hooked her arm into Bobby's.

'Maureen is with me now. There will be no trouble. All that other stuff is in the past.'

'What he's trying to say is that Tommy and me are history. I should have listened to everybody that warned me about him. I'm sorry for what happened to your friend Daniel, that night at Viv's party. I didn't want to come into the Club, he made me. I'm sorry, Jackie. For what it's worth, he always told me that you and him were over when he was with me.'

Jackie paused to think. She was sure that Maureen was lying, that she did know Tommy was attached when they were together. Maureen had a reputation as a bit of slapper. However, Bobby was an old friend of her dad's. She decided to let them in.

'I've got no argument with you now, Maureen, but I will say this: I'd better never find out that you knew about me when that bastard was sleeping with you behind my back.' Jackie snatched the present off Maureen. '...And there's no smoking in the house,' she added.

'I really appreciate this, Jackie,' Bobby grinned. 'See, I told you she was nice!' he said to Maureen. Jackie stood aside to let them in. They piled their coats on top of the other coats on the hooks in the hall. Jackie followed them into the living room.

'What the -' screamed Viv, lifting the needle off the Queen record she was playing. The living room fell silent. Ham rolls and snacks were paused midway to mouths. Mrs Morrisson slowly put the serviettes down. Viv's mum reached for the camera from her knee and switched it to 'on'. Viv's dad sat up in his chair. Father Cleary reached for the peanuts. Frank walked forward.

'Hello, Bobby!' he bellowed, a little too loudly through the silence. 'Glad you could make it. Come in, get yourselves a plate.' He nodded to Maureen, 'Maureen,' he said formally.

'Thank you for welcoming me into your home, Frank. Bobby said you were a kind man.'

Frank nodded again and ushered them to the buffet table. He pointed towards Viv at the record player who had not yet closed her mouth from the shock of seeing Maureen. She adjusted the needle back to the start of the song. People started chatting again. Mrs Morrisson handed Bobby and Maureen plates. Frank felt pleased with himself. *A kind man*, he thought, *that'll do me.* He spotted Jackie on her way to the buffet table.

'You're okay with this, hen? She's all right, really.'

'You should have told me, Dad.'

'But then you would have said they can't come. I want Bobby here, Jackie, he's my pal. And remember what your mum used to say - Nothing unites like a common enemy. Remember? She used to say that all the time. If Tommy knows that you and Maureen are, well, pals now, he might be more inclined to stay away.'

'Well, I suppose her taste in men has improved.'

'Aye. And somebody her own age at last! Try to be happy for Bobby. It's his first girlfriend since... since...wait...is she his first girlfriend? That means Bobby's a-'

'Dad! See if anybody needs a drink. I need to feed the baby.'

'I can do that! Let me do that for you, Jackie.' Mrs Morrisson was there in a flash, arms out for baby June. 'I love feeding her. I've got her a wee plate ready in the kitchen. All her favourite bits. I cut up a crispy pancake! C'mon, hen. You get yourself something too now, Jackie. I know you've only had a vol au vent.'

Viv's dad had made his way over to the hi-fi and lifted the needle off the Queen record. He took *Legs* by ZZ Top from a sleeve and placed it on the turntable. As it started up, he moved his arms like a chicken, keeping his legs still. Viv laughed. 'Don't give him any more whisky, Frank!'

The doorbell rang again. Jackie looked around. Again, nobody heard it. She put her plate down and went to the hall and opened the door.

'Hello there!'

She was delighted to see Daniel, whom she had forgotten was coming, a slight, fair boy beside him.

'Hiya, Daniel!' she hugged him.

'Hiya, Jackie! This is... Johnny. Is it okay if he comes in too? He's brought cans.' Johnny smiled nervously.

'Welcome, Johnny! Of course you can come in.' She closed the door behind them. 'Did anybody ever tell you that you look a wee bit like Jimmy Somerville?'

'I do get that from time to time, aye,' laughed Johnny.

'Just dump your coats anywhere,' said Jackie. She strained to get the living room door open as everybody was up dancing. The crowd let out a loud welcoming roar for Daniel.

'Oh! There he is! The boxer! How's the nose, Daniel, son?' shouted Frank.

'I'm fine, it's all healed now.' Daniel gave Frank the thumbs up. Viv eyed Johnny up and down, then turned back to Daniel.

'Did you bring them?' she asked Daniel. He nodded and handed her some LPs and a few singles. She removed them from the bag.

'Yes! Yes!' she said, 'I've been wanting their new single! That singer! I love him! He's gorgeous!'

'Did you see him on *Top of the Pops*?' asked Johnny. 'He's great isn't he?'

'Aye! Did you see him then? What's your pal's name, Daniel? He's got good taste!'

'Ha ha! I know he has - Viv - this is Johnny.'

'Come on, Johnny, let's see the moves then!' ordered Viv, taking off ZZ Top and putting on The Smiths. Viv's dad sat down next to her mum to watch. The settee was quite deep and he fell backwards into the centre.

'Jesus' sake, I was nearly on the ceiling - watch where you're sitting!' said Viv's mum.

'Sorry, hen. I'll hold your glass for you!' He removed the glass of gin from her hand and pretended to take a sip and laugh. She snatched it back off him. Johnny removed cans of lager from his bag and offered Viv's dad a can off the plastic ring. He took it, cracked it open and swallowed down a few gulps.

'Thirsty work, this dancing!' he said. Just as he was making himself comfortable, The Smiths *Panic* started up to an equal measure of roars of approval and moans of complaint. Viv, Jackie, Daniel and Johnny took the centre place on the carpet and started swinging their arms and swaying.

'Naw, not him, anybody but him!' shouted Frank.

'Are you not a fan, Frank?' asked the priest. 'I quite like a bit of that Morrissey, myself. He's a very clear singer. Crisp. I like to hear every word.'

'Och, well...' replied Frank. He put his drink down. 'I suppose if you can't beat them, Father!'

Frank joined the crowd in the middle of the living room and copied their dance moves. Jackie was bent over at the waist, in a fit of laughter at her dad's antics. She sat down on the armrest of his chair. At the end of the song, everybody flopped down into a seat or onto the floor with exhaustion.

'That was absolutely hilarious!' said Jackie. Mrs Morrisson came back into the room with the baby.

'I think she's ready to go down now, Jackie. Shall I take her up for you? I don't mind.'

'Mrs Morrisson, you're the best!' said Jackie, 'but

wait, I want to say a few words first.' She stood up.

'Are you doing a speech?' asked Frank. The priest clinked his fork against his whisky glass.

'Speech!' called Viv.

'Speech!' called the priest. Everybody joined in, shouting 'Speech!'

Jackie waved her hands for them to stop.

'I just would like to say a few thank you's. First I would like to thank Mrs Morrisson for this fantastic spread she has put on!'

'Round of applause for the tasty buffet!' shouted Frank. Everyone cheered.

'I would also like to thank her for all the help with the baby since she has been born. My mum would be so pleased to know that you are keeping an eye on us all. Thank you for your love and care.'

'It's my pleasure,' blushed Mrs Morrisson. 'Kiss Mummy night night!' Mrs Morrisson leaned the baby in to kiss Jackie. Everybody said good night to baby June and waved like babies. Mrs Morrisson took her up the stairs, content to be needed.

Jackie continued, 'My dad and I would like to thank the Father. Not just for his lovely service but also for all his support... and his guidance... and his home visits. Thank you, Father.' The priest nodded and held up his glass.

'Thank you, Father,' Frank said, quietly. The

priest smiled back at Frank.

'Thanks to Viv for helping me get the baby ready and for always being there for me... and for playing the records tonight!' Some cheers and boos emanated from around the room. Viv smiled, then she scowled, then she smiled again. 'Thanks to everybody who came along today, especially my dad. Dad, I only wish my mum was here to see... to see...' Jackie faded off and started to cry. Frank leaped to her side and handed her his handkerchief.

'And that's the end of the speeches!' he said, abruptly. 'Now, how about somebody for a song?'

'I'll sing but I'm not singing first,' said Viv's dad to Daniel and Johnny, now squashed onto the three seater couch beside him, 'I can't get up!'

'I will offer a little something,' boomed the priest. The room fell silent. He put his glass down and closed his eyes. He extended out his arms as if he was saying Mass and cleared his throat.

'*WHEN THEY BEGIN... THE BEGUINE...*' he bellowed, '*IT BRINGS BACK THE SOUND OF MUSIC SO TENDER...*' Viv's mum nudged Viv's dad and he nudged her back. Jackie cuddled her dad, then retrieved her plate of food and went to sit beside Viv.

The doorbell rang. Frank looked around, nobody else had heard it. He went out to the hall and opened the door to a freezing cold breeze. He hugged his arms around himself. He felt a little light-headed. He looked left and right and down the street.

'Nobody there,' he said, 'I must be hearing things.'

'FRANK! SHUT THE DOOR!' shouted a voice from the party.

He had one last look around and then went back inside, rubbing his shirtsleeves up and down.

'Taken a turn for the cold out there!' he said, closing the door.

Down the street, a lady in a blue coat smiled towards the house. She turned and walked away.

# Author Note

*Frank* was initially a play, entitled *The End Of The Bench*, a comedy about a Scottish character who dreams of an invite to his death from a Game Show Host/Grim Reaper. The character stemmed from a story I heard about a man who attends funerals of people he doesn't know just to get the free steak pie.

Frank became so real I knew I had to write more about him. He seemed a solitary force, so I made him a widower, folding him into some elements of my past: Airdrie, music, family, parties, booze, and, latterly, meat at every meal, an 80s habit that drove me to vegetarianism and, eventually, veganism.

The June 'visits' rest on an observation that when loved ones die, the living lay claim to happenings that keep them close, eg if a robin lands on a bush, a feather floats down, if a song plays, a bee buzzes, people believe these are signs from the deceased.

In Frank's story, the reader must decide if June really is a ghost; or is it Frank's raw grief, or, as one reader put it, is it 'just his age?'

Remember to keep the house tidy, you never know when the priest is coming.

*Julie Hamill*
*August 2017*
🐦 *@juliehamill*
*www.juliehamill.com*

If you enjoyed *Frank,*

Keep an eye open for the second book in the trilogy

*Jackie*

Due out mid-2018

Join our mailing list for advance information:

info@saronpublishers.co.uk

# ABOUT THE AUTHOR

Real name: Julie Patricia Hamill
Birth place/date: Baillieston, December 13th 1971
Birthsign: Sagittarius
Siblings: Rose Ann, Louise, James. All older
Height: virtually and arguably 5 ft 2
Weight: 7 ½ stone
Eyes: blue
Hair: brown
Previous occupations: advertising
Previous bands: Mr Birch and Mr Morris school band (backing singer)
Favourite colour: yellow
Favourite food: artichoke hearts
Favourite drink: ginger beer, lots of ice
Hobbies: Mozarmy. Music, books, jukeboxes, quizzes, dancing, hula hooping
Pets: one schnoodle, Dolly
Ambition in life: to make an album with Louise: *Songs from the dogs*
Self description: an over-flowing cup of fluff
High points of career: meeting Penny Reeves in Cardiff
Favourite book: *15 Minutes With You* by Julie Hamill
Favourite film: *Billy Liar, The Lost Boys, Sid and Nancy, Grease*
Favourite TV programme: *Coronation Street, Mad Men, Sopranos*

# Julie Hamill

TV personality: Terry Wogan
Favourite actors: Tom Hardy, Alison Steadman,
James Gandolfini
Person you would most like to meet: Morrissey
Most important possession: gumption
Most hated record: Midnight Oil: *Beds Are
Burning*
Favourite bands: The Smiths, The Specials,
Depeche Mode
Favourite singer: Morrissey, Kate Bush, Carole
King
Favourite LPs: *World Peace Is None Of Your
Business, Please, Kill Uncle*
Favourite singles: *Velocity Girl, The Rattler,
Promised Land, William, Hit*
First record you ever bought: *The Tide Is High*
First live gig: The Smiths, Glasgow, 1985
Likes: reminiscing with Gillian, Elaine, Jack,
Sharn, Babs & Caroline
Dislikes: itchy labels, meat, cruelty
Favourite animal: dogs
Favourite person: Pat n Jimmy
Heroes: Gerard, Sadie, Archie,
Julie Hes, Neil Wood, Mrs Nelis
Villains: Bernard Matthews
Greatest embarrassment: having to hold my
nose under water
Self confession: I turn the music up when you're
not looking
First romance: Morrissey
Favourite fun thing to do: Visit the Ramada
crazy carpet in West Hollywood

Frank

## Why not try
## *15 Minutes With You*
## by Julie Hamill?

Sickened by blackening reports of Morrissey in the press, Julie Hamill underwent a two-year project interviewing Morrissey associates and famous fans to discover more about pop's most alluring and controversial artist.

*15 Minutes With You* contains twenty-four interviews from band mates to TV stars and beyond. The book reveals a 'behind the scenes' Morrissey; one who is kind, witty, charming and true.

***** 'An absolute must for Morrissey fans. A book of love, not dirt.' *Susanna Walker*

***** 'No hatchet jobs here or trying to score a few points by drawing on any negativity around Morrissey and The Smiths. This book is beautifully put together, encapsulates the years around those who were closest to him.' *The Big O*

***** 'As a lifelong Smiths and book nut, I adore this book. It is beautifully produced, and completely compelling.' -Q*uibbler*

Further interviews can be found on juliehamill.com

Julie Hamill

# ABOUT THE PUBLISHERS

Saron Publishers has been in existence for about ten years, producing niche magazines. Our first venture into books took place in 2016 when we published *The Meanderings of Bing* by Tim Harnden-Taylor. *The Ramblings of Bing* is due out in time for Christmas 2017. *Minstrel Magic* by Eleanor Pritchard came out in June and tells the phenomenal show business story of the George Mitchell Singers and the Black and White Minstrels. Further publications planned for 2017 include *Penthusiasm*, a collection of short stories and poems from a writing group based in the beautiful town of Usk, and *Summer Season* by Rebecca Burton.

Join our mailing list by emailing info@saronpublishers.co.uk. We promise no spam.

Visit our website saronpublishers.co.uk to keep up to date and to read reviews of what we've been reading and enjoying.

Follow us on Facebook @saronpublishers.

Follow us on Twitter @saronpublishers.

Printed in Poland
by Amazon Fulfillment
Poland Sp. z o.o., Wrocław

53787742R00115